THE

GOOD

NEIGHBOR

A.J. BANNER

LAKE UNION
PUBLISHING

Published by Lake Union Publishing, Seattle

www.apub.com

Amazon, the Amazon logo, and Lake Union Publishing are trademarks of Amazon.com, Inc., or its affiliates.

ISBN-13: 9781503944435
ISBN-10: 1503944433

Cover design by Lindsey Andrews

Printed in the United States of America

THE

GOOD

NEIGHBOR

PROLOGUE

I'm drowning. The river's current is tearing me apart. I've kicked off my boots, but my heavy jeans cling to my legs. My chest burns with the need for air. Where is she? I've lost sight of her—no, there she is, too close to the falls. Her head bobs to the surface, her pale face upturned. Her lips are blue.

I strike out after her, but the current yanks me under; I swallow mouthfuls of water. I fight my way upward, break the surface, spitting out mud and silt. The rumble of the waterfall rises to an earsplitting roar.

"I'm coming!" I shout. "Grab on to something!" Is she conscious? Is she even alive? I scream for help, my shrill cries lost in the storm. Right arm, left, reach, pull. My fingers are numb. I can't feel my feet. The sky flashes with lightning, then the crack of thunder, and a familiar voice calls from high on the cliff, a dark figure moving along the embankment.

"*Bon voyage,*" the voice yells in triumph. "Good riddance to both of you."

CHAPTER ONE
TWO MONTHS EARLIER

That early October evening, everything on Sitka Lane was still perfect. The twilight sky blushed in iridescent shades of pink and gold. The first fallen leaves tumbled across the lawn, cedar and alder trees swaying in the ocean breeze. I still felt robust and healthy as I straightened the painting of Miracle Mouse on my studio wall. The furry detective perched on a stack of books, her bespectacled eyes bright and perceptive.

I needed to write her next adventure, but when Johnny went away, I ended up chewing the tip of my pen and staring off into space. Every time my cell phone rang, I imagined his arms around me, his hand at the small of my back, circling lower. After three years of marriage, I still felt like a revved-up newlywed.

I pictured him at his conference in San Francisco, captivated by the latest advances in the treatment of acne and eczema, while I puttered around in the sleepy town of Shadow Cove, Washington, decorating our dream house. Or technically, *Johnny's* dream house, since he'd bought the place before I'd ever met him.

I focused on rearranging my studio, which held the evidence of my busy life—boxes of books to donate to the library, my reading club schedule, notes from writers in my critique group.

At six thirty, my cell phone buzzed, the letters *BFF* popping up on the screen. I hit the answer button. "I thought you and Dan had left for India."

"Our flight's in four hours," Natalie replied, Miles Davis playing in the background. "I had a weird feeling about you."

"What is it now?" Natalie was the queen of outlandish premonitions. Ten years earlier, when we'd met as undergrads, she'd predicted the apocalypse before every exam.

"I worry one of those tall trees will fall on your roof."

"You get this way before you travel," I said.

"I know, but you're alone in that gigantic house, and—"

"It's not so gigantic." It was true, but still, I shivered. The wind picked up outside, rushing through the trees. "I still can't believe you'll be gone for six months."

"The clinic wanted Dan for a year, but his patients need him here. I'll bring you some silk and sandalwood."

"And Darjeeling tea," I said.

"Green tea is better for your health, if you're trying to get preggers."

"I prefer black tea. You know that." I felt a twinge beneath my ribs. Johnny and I had been trying to conceive for nearly a year.

"One cup a day," Natalie said. "Or drink decaf."

"Yeah, yeah. Do you ever stop being a nutritionist?"

"Only in my sleep. Give that hunky husband a hug for me."

"Likewise." I hung up, missing Natalie already. As I finished tidying my desk, her words played through my mind. *I had a weird feeling . . .*

A few minutes later, my phone rang again, the word *Johnny* lighting the screen in blocky white letters.

"I missed you all day, Dr. McDonald," I said, smiling.

"I missed you more," he replied in his sleepy baritone voice. "I've been up to my ears in hidradenitis suppurativa—"

"Suppura-what?"

"It's associated with high morbidity."

"I hate that word, *morbidity*. Sounds like death."

"It *is* about death. I need to come home."

"You mean you're not turned on by exciting lectures on flesh-eating bacteria?"

"I'm turned on by you. What are you wearing?"

"That little lace number you got me for Christmas," I lied, looking down at my T-shirt and denim coveralls.

"Mmm. We could, you know . . . over the phone."

"Wait a minute. Someone's at the Kimballs' house." A car rumbled up the neighbors' driveway, the engine kicking off.

"They're allowed to have guests."

"But the Kimballs are in Hawaii. They asked me to keep an eye on their house. Hang on." I headed for the kitchen, pulled up the blinds. In the darkening twilight, two figures emerged from a station wagon in the neighbors' driveway. Only a narrow strip of lawn separated their house from ours. I recognized Chad Kimball, thick and stocky, built like a football player except for his sloping shoulders. Monique resembled Marilyn Monroe in a striking way, curvy and breathless, with her shimmering blue dress flapping against her legs.

But where was Mia? Probably asleep in her car seat. "It's them," I said, letting the blinds drop. "They're back early. Maybe Mia got sick. I'll talk to Monique in the morning."

Johnny yawned. "G'night, my sweet. I love you only."

"Me, too. I love you only." I hung up and finished tidying my desktop. Miracle Mouse watched me from the wall, every brushstroke of her fur lovingly painted by my grandmother. Nana had given me the picture when my first Miracle Mouse mystery had been accepted for publication. Now Nana was gone, but her memory haunted Miracle's discerning gaze. As usual, I touched Miracle's nose before retiring for the night.

On my way upstairs, I heard the melodic tones of the doorbell. I found Monique Kimball standing on the porch, the wind blowing white-blond hair across her face. At close range, her movie-star features came into focus—pouty lips, expressive gray eyes, and thick, curved lashes. Her skin was lightly tanned, a sprinkling of freckles on her cheeks. The faint smells of travel rose from her—airplane, sweat, and expensive perfume.

"You're back early," I said. "Is everything okay?"

She smiled wanly. "It's complicated. But I didn't come over to complain. Could I borrow a bag of charcoal?"

"Come on back. We've got a bag on the deck."

Monique stepped inside and followed me down the hall. As we passed through the family room, she whistled in delight. "*Oh la la!* I love the way you've redecorated. Is the blue couch new?"

"I got rid of that old black monstrosity. It screamed 'bachelor pad.'"

"You've really fixed up the place."

"Thanks, it's been fun." When I'd moved in, I'd added silk throw pillows, lavender sachets, scented soaps. I had a few nice pieces of furniture made from sustainably harvested wood, including a pearl diver chest in the hall.

Out on the windy back deck, a lawn chair lay on its side, and a garden rake had toppled over. I picked up a small bag of charcoal and handed it to Monique. "Sure you can get a barbecue going in this weather?"

"You know my husband. He likes a challenge." Monique tucked the bag under her arm. Back in the foyer, she hesitated. "Jules is okay? He's gone to bed early?" She gazed up the staircase, as if she might want to borrow Johnny as well. Occasionally, she reverted to calling him "Jules" and her husband "Jim," after characters in *Jules and Jim*, a French movie the four of us had watched together, about two men in love with the same woman. But Monique and I had argued about who most resembled the *femme fatale*, Catherine.

"Another conference," I said. "How's Jim?"

"Tired and sunburned. His skin is too sensitive." Monique seemed about to say something more, but instead she turned to peek out through the narrow window next to the front door. Across the street, Jessie Ramirez sat on her front steps in a sweatshirt and jeans, her dark hair whipping across her face. A tall boy sat next to her, dressed in a hoodie and smoking—her new boyfriend, Adrian, his low-rider black Buick parked in the driveway.

Monique frowned. "Why does she hang out with him?"

"She's seventeen, the age of raging hormones. But she's a good kid."

"She takes good care of our house when we're away, but . . ."

"But what?"

"I kept a gold pen by the phone, and now I can't find it. Maybe it fell behind the fridge."

"You think she stole it?"

"I'm sure it'll turn up. Please don't mention it to her."

"Don't worry. My lips are sealed."

Monique left in a rush, hips swaying as she crossed the narrow strip of lawn toward her front door. Jessie and the boy watched her go. Jessie had been a model student before she'd taken up with Adrian. But even now, I couldn't imagine the girl stealing from anyone. She'd always been helpful and honest, but who knew the deeper mind of a teenager?

The house to the right of Jessie's was dark. Felix and Maude Calassis had probably gone to bed early, although Felix often walked at dusk.

Beyond the Calassis place, the porch light shone at the empty house on the corner. The Realtor, Eris Coghlan, had forgotten to switch off the light. A SOLD plaque overlaid the FOR SALE sign posted in the yard.

To the left of Jessie's house, beyond a dense stand of firs, the Frenkels kept an immaculate home at the end of the cul-de-sac. Lenny Frenkel stood on the front porch, cell phone plastered to his ear. He was the thinner of the Frenkel twins, a charming fast talker. Several girls had already asked him to the senior prom. Lukas, the thicker twin, resembled his father, Verne—brawny and shy.

On a street like Sitka Lane, with only six spacious, identical houses, it was difficult—but not impossible—to keep secrets. I could watch the neighbors come and go, but nobody knew what truly went on inside each home.

Upstairs in the master bathroom, I could smell Johnny's pine-scented aftershave and his favorite shea butter soap. I changed from my coveralls into one of his extra-long T-shirts and opened the window before climbing into bed. The scents of night drifted in—salty sea air, astringent cedar, and the honey-scented flowers of the bugbane plant beneath the window. I tried to focus on reading *Your Healthy Pregnancy*, but the words blurred across the page. Didn't prehistoric parents already know what to do without a book? Didn't they trust their instincts? They weren't sitting in their caves, reading how-to manuals around the fire. But then, too many newborns must've died back then, before the age of modern medicine.

The murmur of voices drifted up from the Kimballs' backyard, mingling with the smell of barbecued hot dogs. After a time, their patio doors slid open and shut, followed by a quiet interlude. Heaviness lingered in the air, like the threat of a coming storm.

I lay back and closed my eyes, but sleep eluded me. The wind whipped through the fir branches, and beneath the wind came the deep rumble of an engine prowling up the street. The motor cut off, and silence followed. Probably teenagers making out. It was way past their bedtime, and way past mine.

Finally, I slipped into a restless slumber, only to awaken in darkness. The gale rattled the window, and a loud sound echoed in my ears, maybe a truck backfiring. The digital clock on the nightstand read 1:17 a.m. Diffuse orange light played across the walls; the smell of smoke wafted through the air.

I switched on the bedside lamp, and the room rushed into view: my favorite wedding photo on the bureau, sweatshirt draped across a chair, lotion bottles on the dresser. Nothing appeared amiss, but my heart thumped erratically. I got up and peered out the window. It took a moment for the scene to register in my sleepy brain. Smoke and flames billowed from the house next door, from the Kimballs' first-floor windows. Their fire alarm kicked on—a high-pitched beeping. A child's terrified cries pierced the night. Mia. She was trapped in her bedroom on the second floor, right above a raging fire.

CHAPTER TWO

I grabbed my cell phone from the nightstand, punched in 911. My fingers trembled; I thought I might faint. An operator's nasal voice came on the line. "Shadow Cove 911, where's your emergency?"

"My neighbors' house is on fire! Hurry! Their little girl—"

"What's your name, ma'am?"

"Sarah Phoenix. My neighbors are the Kimballs, Chad and Monique. Their daughter, Mia. She's only four. She's crying in her room—"

"What is their address, ma'am?"

"Theirs is 595 Sitka Lane. We're in 599, right next door. Hurry."

"Help is on the way."

"How long will it take?"

"First responders are en route from the central station."

Fifteen minutes away. I hung up, dialed the Kimballs' number, got a fast busy signal.

I couldn't wait around. I yanked on my sweats and sneakers, dropped my cell phone in my pocket, and ran out into the hall. Halfway down the stairs, I tripped, tumbled down the steps, and landed sprawled out in the foyer. Stupid, stupid. People tripped this way only in the movies.

In a moment, I was back on my feet, and out of habit, I snatched my purse from the table and flung the strap over my shoulder on my way out the door.

Towering cedars swayed against the blustery night. The fire crackled and roared like a living creature. The neighborhood glowed in an orange-tinted tableau of shadows, the air thick with the acrid stench of burning wood and plastic. The Kimballs' alarm still shrieked, and Mia's plaintive cries drifted through a haze of smoke. Voices yelled across the street; doors opened and slammed.

The entire first floor of the Kimballs' house was engulfed in flames. Jessie's parents, Don and Pedra Ramirez, raced over in their night-clothes. Jessie followed in jeans and a hoodie. The neighborhood converged on the Kimballs' lawn. Felix and Maude Calassis were there, and the Frenkels with their twin teenaged sons in pajamas. Don tried the Kimballs' front door, but it was locked. Lukas Frenkel strode up the steps and kicked in the door, then stumbled backward, coughing in a cloud of smoke. Lenny turned on the garden hose and shot a jet of water toward the blaze.

"I called 911," Orla Frenkel yelled above the din, her angular face tight with worry. Her flimsy silk negligee fluttered in the wind.

"Me, too," I shouted back. "We need to get inside!"

"We can't go in the front," Lukas said, still coughing.

"But Mia!" I said. "Chad and Monique—where are they?"

"They're still inside!" Don yelled. He and Verne Frenkel ran around to the other side of the house. Lenny kept hosing the front, but the thin stream of water seemed only to feed the flames.

I rushed to the back deck, yanked at the sliding glass door. Locked. I peered through narrow slats in the blinds. Flames and smoke filled the family room. Through the haze, I glimpsed the kitchen window, which appeared to be shattered, as if someone had hurled a rock through the glass.

"Don't go in there!" Orla said behind me, tugging my sleeve. "It's not safe."

We sprinted back to the side of the house where Mia's second-floor room faces my room. Pedra Ramirez approached in a flapping white robe and pink slippers. "*Díos mio*. Where are the Kimballs? Sarah! Where's Johnny?"

"San Francisco," I said, breathless. How had my sweats become damp?

Jessie had turned on our front faucet and dragged the hose across the Kimballs' driveway, shooting a useless stream of water toward the fire.

Don jogged up to us, his face sooty and grim. "We can't find a safe way in. I called 911 again. Responders are eight minutes out."

How could so little time have passed? I pointed up at Mia's bedroom window. "Get a ladder. Hurry!"

"You can't go up there," Pedra said, her eyes wide.

"We've got a ladder," Don shouted. He and Jessie raced back across the street to their house.

I pulled the phone from my pocket, called Johnny's cell. No answer, so I dialed information for his hotel and reached a perky-voiced woman at the front desk. "Give me Dr. Johnny McDonald's room. It's urgent."

"Hold on, please. I'll try that extension." But the phone kept ringing in Johnny's room. The clerk's voice came back on the line. "He's not picking up. I'll put you through to his voice mail."

I left him a frantic message and hung up, just as Don and Jessie returned with the ladder. Don propped it against the side of the Kimballs' house, below Mia's window. A group of neighbors gathered around; others dragged more garden hoses across the street, shooting crisscrossing arcs of water at the flames.

"Hold the ladder," I said, my heart racing. I slipped my cell phone into my purse, handed the purse to Pedra.

"*You're* not going up," Don said.

"I can fit through the window," I said.

"So can I," Jessie said.

"You stay here. Don't argue." I elbowed my way to the ladder, grabbed a brick from the Kimballs' side garden, and dropped it in my sweatshirt pocket as I climbed.

"Wait!" Pedra shouted. "Let Don go instead."

"I'm fine!" I yelled down. "See if there's another way in, something we missed."

"We're on it," Don said, and ran around back again.

Verne Frenkel stepped forward and held the ladder in place. "Steady as she goes," he said.

"Be careful up there," Jessie shouted.

"Don't let go of the ladder." I kept my gaze trained upward. My knees turned to rubber, the palms of my hands sweaty. I clenched my teeth, determined to ignore my fear of heights. Smoke thickened in the air, stinging my eyes and making me cough.

At the top, I found Mia's window open a few inches but locked in place. Inside, a night-light revealed the shapes of a dresser, a rocking chair, and a single bed. But no Mia. The alarm had gone silent. A sliver of light glowed around the frame of the bedroom door. The fire seethed on the other side, a monster trying to gain entry.

"Mia, where are you?" I shouted through the screen.

A small form crawled out from behind the bed. "I'm right here. I want my mommy!"

"Don't move. I'm coming for you." I popped out the screen. "Watch out below!" I dropped the screen to the ground. "Stay out of the way, honey."

Mia cringed, crawling backward.

Holding the ladder with my left hand, I swung the brick in my right, broke a hole in the glass. I tossed the brick into Mia's room, onto the floor, then reached in and unlocked the window. In a moment, I stood inside the room, a blanket of heat pressing on me. I stepped over crunching broken glass and scooped Mia into my arms. She felt much heavier than her thirty pounds. "Hold on around my neck. Don't let go."

She nearly strangled me with her grip. Two more steps and we reached the bedroom door, the heat almost blasting us backward. "Chad! Monique!" I yelled. No answer. "I have Mia!" Still, no reply.

I headed back to the window and climbed over the sill, a tricky maneuver with a child in my arms. "I have her!" I shouted. "Coming down!"

"We've got you!" Verne called up. "Hurry."

On the way down the ladder, Mia grew heavier by the moment, although she was small for her age.

"Mommy," she whimpered. "My Cinderella shoes."

"We can get you new ones," I said. Where were Chad and Monique? I hoped that Don had found them, that they had escaped.

"I'm scared," Mia whispered, looking into my eyes.

"Me, too. But we're going to be okay." I clamped Mia's small body between my arms, hoping not to drop her. The nauseating stink of burning chemicals blew through the air, and suddenly, something exploded overhead. A tempest of debris rained down through the smoke. Flames shot from Mia's window, embers catching an updraft and landing on our roof, igniting the cedar shingles.

Jessie was shouting below. "Your house is on fire. Sarah, hurry!"

In an instant, crazy thoughts raced through my mind. *My manuscript, the wedding photos, my journal, legal papers, passports. The painting of Miracle Mouse. Kamba wood carvings from my mother in the Peace Corps in Kenya. My wedding band on the dresser.* I always took off my ring at night. I had to get back into the house, but I couldn't rush.

Five more rungs and we reached solid ground. As I transferred Mia into Pedra's arms, the wail of sirens approached in the distance. The fire had flared across our roof. The master bedroom lit up from within, illuminated in a dreamlike glow I could see through the skylight. More debris pelted down, and when I looked upward, a large black object was hurtling toward me in slow motion, a meteor, space wreckage tumbling end over end, down and down, and then I saw nothing at all.

CHAPTER THREE

I woke up in a drab gray room, a mask pressed to my face, feeding me moist oxygen. I reached up to touch my painful forehead, felt a rough bandage against my fingers. My head throbbed as if a concrete high-rise had fallen on my skull. Something pulled at the back of my hand, an IV dripping fluids into my veins. I wore a soft cotton hospital gown and socks beneath a crisp sheet and blanket. Where were my clothes? Where was my purse? I'd handed it off to Pedra.

I could make out an open door to a tiny bathroom, a window overlooking the woods, a metal countertop on which a paper coffee cup sat, the blue Shadow Café logo printed on the side.

Which hospital was this? How long had I been unconscious? By the angle of pale sunlight, I was sure it must be afternoon. A distant voice echoed on an intercom, soft-soled shoes squeaked past the room, and even through the mask, I smelled rubbing alcohol and other medicinal odors.

A deep, familiar voice spoke in a hushed tone just outside the door. I tried to sit up, but my limbs felt leaden. A few words drifted in here and there.

". . . need to stay with her," a man said. "I don't know how long. She's my *wife*."

I pulled off the mask and called out, "Johnny!" My voice came out weak and raspy, but somehow he heard me. He strode into the room, dropping the cell phone into his coat pocket. Beneath the unzipped jacket, he wore a rumpled white dress shirt, and he had on black slacks, his dark hair a mess, his face pale and drawn. Despite his disheveled appearance, he gave off a forceful masculinity, a mesmerizing charisma. His brilliant blue eyes were filled with concern as he leaned over the bed and hugged me.

"Sarah," he said. He kissed my cheek, my lips, and I reached my arms around his neck. How I'd missed the feel of him, the scent of pine on his skin.

"Where am I?" I whispered in his ear.

"You're in Cove Hospital. You've got a concussion. You were hit by falling timber."

Last thing I remembered, I'd been handing off Mia to Pedra. "How long have I been here?"

He checked his wristwatch, the silver band shiny in the light. "It's almost two o'clock." He sat in the chair by the bed, still holding my hand.

I felt like a dry leaf about to blow away. "The Kimballs? Chad and Monique?"

"They . . ." His words died, his eyes full of pain.

"What are you saying?"

He shook his head, squeezing my hand. His bereft expression told me everything. I went numb, my mind grasping for an image of Monique—her vibrant smile, her shimmering dress, everything about her in fluid motion. "No. It can't be true."

"I'm so sorry," Johnny whispered.

I drew a shuddering breath, tears slipping down my cheeks. A mundane memory came to me, of Chad brushing pepper off a salmon steak that Monique had marinated for the barbecue. Chad hated pepper. How could it be that they were both gone? "What about Mia?"

"She's okay."

"But she's an orphan now. She—"

"She's with her grandmother." He climbed onto the bed beside me, his weight depressing the thin hospital mattress. He pulled me into his arms.

"What about everyone else?"

"The neighbors? Everyone's okay. I sent a message to your mom. She's driving to Nairobi, to a phone."

"I don't want her to worry—"

"You know she will." He handed me a crumpled tissue from his pocket. "What the hell happened?"

I wiped my cheeks. "I have no idea. Everything was fine . . . A noise woke me up."

"What kind of noise?"

"An explosion or something. What about our house?"

He interlaced his fingers with mine. "Badly damaged. Okay, ruined."

"Everything? But the firefighters were on their way—"

"The second floor was already in flames. They couldn't save it. At least, the house is not habitable."

I remembered burning embers carried on the wind. But how could our entire home be lost? Monique and Chad dead? The room shrank; voices in the hall grated against my eardrums. "When can we go back? I need to see—"

"You need to stay here for a couple of days. We can go back when we know your head is okay."

I let out a dry, mirthless laugh. "My head will never be okay, ever again."

"I'm so sorry." His pocket emitted a low buzzing sound. He pulled out his cell phone, glanced at the screen, then tucked the phone back into his pocket. "Homeowners' insurance. I'll call them back later."

"You're already talking to them?" But of course he was. Johnny had always been efficient. He thought ahead, a trait I admired in him.

"I had to make sure we have rental coverage for temporary housing," he said. "I've been talking to Puget Sound Energy, the county PUD. The power and water were shut off. Everything's gone."

But no, not everything. Not our memories, not my perfect recall of the first time I'd stepped inside Johnny's house. He'd invited me over for dinner, our second date, and he'd bought my favorite outdoor plant, a potted turquoise hydrangea. He'd forgotten to remove the price tag. But he'd melted my heart with his efforts to impress me, especially when he'd burned the lasagna. We'd ended up sharing peanut butter sandwiches by candlelight. I'd laughed at his jokes, told him about Miracle Mouse. He'd listened with rapt attention, watching my lips, sending waves of heat through me, his long-lashed eyes full of intent. And soon, the small talk had ceased. Now we would have to hold on to the memories—they were all we had to keep us going.

CHAPTER FOUR

My body and brain needed time to recover, the neurologist said. He was a birdlike man with large spectacles and a receding hairline. He repeated what Johnny had told me already: I'd suffered a concussion, a mild form of brain injury. I was under observation for a couple of days. I might experience headaches, dizziness, temporary loss of short-term memory.

That night, I drifted in and out of shallow, restless sleep. Whenever I awoke in a sweat, half-remembered dreams lingered at the edge of my mind. No, not dreams. Nightmares. Flashes of fire, falling timbers, the glow around Mia's bedroom door. Sometimes I dreamed we were home again, the white bugbane flowers glowing in the moonlight, Monique standing on the porch, her hair blowing across her face.

Johnny grieved in his own quiet way. He slept on the hospital bed beside me, his body pressed against mine, ignoring the guest cot the nurse had unfolded for him. In the morning, he got up early and showered in the tiny bathroom. His suitcase sat on a fold-out table, still holding his conference wear: suits, ties, dress socks.

He ventured out to take care of business, returning with ill-fitting clothes for me, toiletries, and magazines. Thankful for my intact cell phone, I checked my voice mail and returned calls from friends, including a tearful message from Natalie, who had arrived in New Delhi. "I'm coming home," she said. "Didn't I say this would happen? Didn't I?"

"It wasn't a tree falling on the house," I told her.

"But something hit you in the head. Could've been a tree branch."

"I suppose, but—"

"This isn't over yet. I feel something worse coming on. Only this time it's not going to be a tree or a fire. It's going to be less obvious, something insidious."

"You watch too many scary movies," I said. "You and Dan enjoy India. I'll see you in a few months." I hung up before she could protest. Then I called my editor, and when I claimed to be all right, someone else spoke through me, another Sarah, a shadow envoy created to fool the world.

My mother telephoned a few hours later when she reached Nairobi. Her distant voice echoed across the continents. "I've been worried about you."

"I'm fine," I lied. My head still hurt, my thoughts fuzzy.

"Why don't you go home? You can stay there as long as you want. Your room is made up. There's a key under the turtle stone."

She'd bought the gray stone turtle right before my father had moved out. I'd been nine years old. My mother and I had stayed in the house, a Craftsman-style bungalow in Portland, Oregon, until I'd left home at eighteen. Suddenly, I longed for my childhood bedroom with its serene view of a wooded ravine.

"Sweet of you to offer," I said. "But it's too far away. We'll find something here. It's going to take a while to get back on our feet."

"I'll come back."

"No need. We're okay." My mother would only get in the way. She would try to be helpful, but I would sense her itch to travel, and she was doing more good in her village in Kenya, where she taught sign language to deaf children.

"I love you," my mother said, a catch in her voice.

"I love you, too." I hung up, tears in my eyes.

A series of visitors followed, including Pedra and Jessie Ramirez, who brought a vase of multicolored flowers and a greeting card with a picture of Wonder Woman on the front. The message inside read,

Kind and caring,

kick-butt, too,

saving little Mia,

that is you.

Nearly everyone on Sitka Lane had signed the card.

Come back to us soon. You're a hero. We love you.

I dissolved into tears. I didn't feel like a hero. What if I'd climbed the ladder sooner? Could I have rescued Chad and Monique as well? What was done was done. Pedra, Jessie, and I cried together in my hospital room, holding one another, grateful for what had been saved, grieving for what had been lost.

***

The next afternoon, while Johnny was out, the doctor returned to my room one last time before discharging me. He performed a quick neurological exam, testing my reflexes and responses—touch, hearing, smell, taste, sight.

Was I no longer physically myself? Could I not trust my senses? Maybe not. I'd awoken in the night and spotted a silhouette in the doorway, the shape of a man, but Johnny had been in the bed beside me, snoring softly. Terrified, I'd squeezed my eyes shut, and when I'd opened them a minute later, the man had disappeared. Perhaps I'd been dreaming. Or hallucinating.

After the doctor tested my balance and strength, he gave me a pass to leave the hospital. "But you need to rest," he said. "No strenuous physical or mental activity for a while."

"I have a new book coming out. I've got signings scheduled—"

"Cancel them."

"But it's the way I make a living." I couldn't turn off my mind. In fact, my neurons and synapses felt more active than usual.

"At least for a few weeks." And then he was gone, as Johnny returned with shopping bags, which he placed on the counter next to a smattering of gifts from friends.

"I'm free," I said. "Let's go to the house."

Johnny's eyes darkened. "Remember, there is no house."

"Still, I need to see."

"If you say so. Don't go anywhere. I'll be right back." He left his cell phone on the counter, went into the bathroom, and shut the door. A moment later, his phone buzzed. *Unknown Number* flashed on the screen. I answered, "Hello? This is Dr. McDonald's—"

A dial tone blared in my ear. The words *CALL ENDED* lit the screen in bright red letters. I heard the toilet flush, and Johnny came out. "Who called?" he said, washing his hands at the sink.

"I don't know. They hung up."

His lips turned down, his brow furrowed. "That's odd. I've had a few hang-ups lately." He tore a paper towel from the roll and dried his hands.

"Someone stalking you?" I put the phone on the counter.

"Happens sometimes. They'll give up, eventually." He threw the paper towel in the trash, stood behind me, and wrapped his arms around my waist, both of us gazing into the mirror. He looked gaunt, with new worry lines next to his eyes. He'd been working too hard, not sleeping enough.

"I'm well enough to help you now," I said, reaching up to touch the stubble on his cheek. "You don't have to take care of everything."

"I don't mind. Doc said you need to rest."

"We can still make decisions together." But he was right. I barely recognized my reflection in the mirror—sallow skin, sunken eyes, limp hair. In the author photo printed in my books, my shiny hair bounced around my shoulders and I looked radiant, alive.

"We need to decide where we're going," Johnny said.

"Home. I want to go home." I leaned back against his chest, an ache of nostalgia in my bones.

Johnny kissed the top of my head. "We can't sleep in the ruins." But I wanted to. By sheer force of will, I would make the ashes rise and reconstitute themselves into the familiar objects of home.

I turned to gaze up into his eyes. "I know it's going to be hard, but—"

"We can start again in a new place," Johnny said. "We could move to that town that gets rain year-round. Forks, where they filmed those vampire movies. It's so wet there, nothing ever catches fire."

"You've got obligations. The clinic."

"I'll move the clinic."

"Your patients can't move with you. They rely on you."

"Shhh." Johnny touched his finger to my lips. "Let's talk about this later. For now, I've got us a rental on the other side of town."

"So that's where you've been all day."

"Not *all* day."

Close up, his face came into focus—his thick lashes, the barely noticeable white birthmark on his forehead, the stubble on his jaw.

"How did you find a place so quickly?"

"I ran into Maude. She was out hosing debris off her lawn. She said Eris Coghlan owns a rental across town. You know, the Realtor?

So I gave her a call. Turns out she has a cottage, half-furnished but unoccupied. We can move in anytime. It's on a quiet dead-end street."

"You've been there already?" My head began to spin again. Johnny worked so efficiently. Usually, I appreciated knowing he'd covered all the bases. I was thankful for a place to stay, so why did uneasiness tug at me? Perhaps because Johnny and I were homeless, forced to rely on the kindness of strangers.

"I checked out the cottage, yeah," he said. "It's small, but it has a certain charm. After we stop by Sitka Lane, I'll drive you out there. You can take a look and decide for yourself."

"I'm sure it will be perfect," I said. The sanctuary would be a blessing. Change was born of necessity. I had to be practical now.

CHAPTER FIVE

On the drive back to Sitka Lane, I watched pedestrians strolling along the brick sidewalks of Waterfront Road, peering in shop windows and sipping iced coffees, as if their lives would always be normal. Dry leaves skittered along the gutters, maples turning deep shades of gold and crimson. Autumn was showing off, but sooner or later, autumn would turn into winter, and the trees would lose all their leaves.

Johnny drove west through the old part of town, populated by Victorian homes built during the heyday of the timber industry a century earlier. At nearly seven o'clock, the moon rose behind us, the sunset a smudge of pink across the western horizon. As Johnny turned onto Sitka Lane, my heart fluttered with nervousness. What would remain of the two houses? Johnny parked at the curb and held my hand.

The damage was worse than I'd expected. How could this horrible mess have once been our home? Blasted-out windows, blackened siding streaked with water damage, the roof caved in. The yard resembled a garbage dump surrounded by yellow FIRE LINE tape. The stink of burned wood and fabric remained in the air.

Next door, only a shell of the Kimballs' house remained. Two suited investigators picked their way through the rubble. The neighborhood was otherwise quiet, shadowed by tall firs, but I sensed people peering out their windows. The night of the fire rushed back to me—the flames, the smoke. Chad and Monique trapped inside their house, slowly suffocating.

"Earth to Sarah. Where are you?" Johnny's voice echoed down a long tunnel.

"I'm here," I said, but in my mind, I was back on the ladder with Mia in my arms. "Let's go."

"You don't want to see—?"

"Not now."

Johnny pulled away from the curb. "I shouldn't have brought you here."

"I wanted to come. I should've done more that night—"

"You did everything you could."

I nodded, not trusting myself to speak without dissolving into tears. As Johnny drove back through town, retracing our route, I opened the window and inhaled the fresh air. He headed east into a heavily wooded area and turned onto a narrow, forested road. The street sign read SHADOW BLUFF LANE, and a smaller sign read DEAD END—NO OUTLET. He slowed past an imposing white Victorian mansion with pale green trim. In the driveway, men in coveralls packed equipment into a blue truck.

"That's Eris Coghlan's place," Johnny said.

I leaned out the window for a better look. "She lives alone?"

"Yeah. Divorced. Not sure about kids." To the left, across the road, lay an expanse of dense forest.

He kept driving past another grove of tall fir trees and pointed out a moss-colored cottage on the right, set back from the road and surrounded by a buffer of forest. "That's the rental."

"You found us a fairy tale," I said as he parked in the driveway. Through the trees, another neighbor's house appeared at the end of the cul-de-sac—a modern cedar A-frame with large windows.

Johnny's shoulders relaxed. "Are you sure? Be honest. We can still go to a hotel."

"I am being honest."

"It has only two bedrooms, one bath—"

"Do we need more than that? I lived in a rented room in college. It was good enough then, and it's more than good enough now."

"It's bigger than a room, at least." He got out of the car and retrieved our meager luggage from the trunk, leaving the gifts in the backseat. Together we climbed the creaky wooden steps to the rickety porch. Birds twittered in the trees, and some larger animal disturbed the nearby underbrush. In the distance, a river rushed down from the foothills of the Olympic Mountains.

Johnny slid the key into the lock. The door swung open, and he heaved the suitcases inside and dropped them in the foyer. Then he leaned back against the open door. "This is it. What do you think?"

I stepped inside. The entryway opened into a well-lit living room painted in pale yellow, oak floors recently swept. Underneath the smells of cleaners and polish, I detected the subtle odors of decay, of old wood. A bay window, with a diagonal hairline crack in the glass, revealed a view of a grassy lawn, a tire swing hanging from a large fir tree, and a forest beyond.

Johnny wrapped his arms around my waist from behind, his firm chest pressed against my back, and I gave in to his warmth. He touched his lips to the sensitive spot at the base of my neck, and I inhaled sharply. He knew me so well. I turned to face him, and he kissed me, his lips firm and insistent. There was something electric about him, a subcurrent of energy. A subtle, unfamiliar scent rose from him— maybe sandalwood. A new aftershave?

"Excuse me? Dr. McDonald?" a mellifluous voice interrupted. "Oh, I'm sorry to intrude. I'll come back later."

"Oh no, excuse us," I said, stepping back, my cheeks flushed. Eris Coghlan stood on the porch, athletic and elegant in jeans, sneakers, and a turquoise short-sleeved shirt. I recognized her from the many times I'd seen her on Sitka Lane, showing the house on the corner, but I'd never spoken to her. Her shiny, russet hair fell in soft waves to her shoulders. She stood straight and strong, projecting a winning combination of ambition and approachability.

Johnny reached out to shake hands with her. "Eris. This is my wife, Sarah."

"Pleased to meet you," Eris said, shaking my hand with cool fingers.

"I've heard a lot about you," I said.

"All good things, I hope." Eris laughed smoothly—a genuine, unaffected sound.

"Fabulous things. Congratulations on selling the house on Sitka Lane."

"The house sold itself. Beautiful construction on a beautiful street." Her eyes darkened. "I'm so sorry about the fire."

I nodded, dryness returning to my throat. "Thank you."

Johnny's face was blank, but I recognized the slight twitch of his eyelid.

Eris smiled. "Pedra Ramirez says you're an author under your maiden name . . . ?"

"Phoenix," I said, relieved to change the subject.

"I hope you find some quiet time here, for your writing. Would you like a tour of the cottage?"

"That would be wonderful." I stepped aside and Eris strode past me, leaving a trail of subtle perfume in her wake. She showed us the quirks of the cottage, from the finicky thermostat in the living room, to the stuck window in the kitchen and the temperamental flush in the bathroom. "I'll get my guy to fix everything. I wasn't expecting tenants."

"It's perfect," I said. "Thank you for renting to us on short notice."

"Wish I could do more to help." She showed us the back master bedroom with its queen-sized bed and two nightstands, then the front bedroom, which she had converted into an office with desk, shelves, and a recliner in the corner. Through the window, I spotted a woman traipsing up the driveway in a black hooded coat, holding an envelope.

Eris glanced outside. "I wonder what she wants." The woman came up to the porch and pulled off the hood. Her beauty took my breath away. She resembled a young Elizabeth Taylor, black-haired and ivory-skinned, exotic and voluptuous.

Eris ushered the woman inside. "Theresa Minkowski, meet your new neighbors. Johnny McDonald and Sarah Phoenix."

"Pleasure," Johnny said. He shook Theresa's hand, his grip lingering a moment too long. A shadow of recognition crossed his face, but he gave no indication that he knew her. Perhaps she'd been a patient. He'd treated nearly everyone in town for one skin ailment or another.

"Welcome to the neighborhood." Theresa withdrew her hand and shook mine. Her fingers felt warm, pliant.

"We're married," I offered. "Johnny and I."

"But with different surnames," Eris said.

Theresa smiled. "I took my husband's name. He and our son are both named Kadin. We live in the A-frame down the street."

"There you have it," Eris said.

Theresa handed the envelope to Eris. "We got your mail again."

"Oh, dear. I have to tell the new carrier." As Eris tucked the envelope into her pocket, I glimpsed part of the return address, *Attorneys at Law.*

Theresa smiled at me. "We'll be seeing you both tomorrow, then?"

"Tomorrow?" Johnny caught her gaze.

Eris laughed. "She beat me to it. I've been meaning to invite you both for dinner."

"We appreciate the offer, but . . ." I looked at Johnny, hoping for a way out. I didn't have the energy to socialize.

He nodded and smiled. "Sure, yeah. Our cupboards are bare."

"But . . ." I began.

"Good," Eris said. "Around seven."

"See you then," Theresa said, stepping out onto the porch. "Looks like you've got another visitor."

A truck marked "County Fire Marshal" crept up the driveway and parked behind Johnny's RAV4. My stomach turned to nervous mush. I wasn't ready to relive the fire, to answer questions, but it seemed I would have no choice.

CHAPTER SIX

"Ryan Greene," the fire marshal said in a deep, resonant voice. Tablet computer in hand, he stood a few inches taller than Johnny, who approached six feet. I couldn't help staring at the man's features, the stereotype of rugged handsomeness beneath cropped auburn hair—square jaw, a slight bump on his nose, and a strong, athletic build, as if he lifted weights and climbed mountains as well (perhaps at the same time). Eris and Theresa had made a hasty exit.

My cheeks flushed, and I forced a smile. "Sarah Phoenix."

He shook my hand in an almost disabling grip. "Sorry for your loss, ma'am. How're you holding up?" He let go of my hand and looked at my forehead. I touched the bandage self-consciously.

"Better, thanks." *Better* was a relative term.

"Get you anything?" Johnny said. "Gourmet glass of tap water? We need to make a grocery run."

"I'm good," Mr. Greene said. "Where can we talk?"

I gestured toward the living room, and we all went inside, the wooden floor creaking beneath our feet.

Mr. Greene sank into the couch. The computer rested on his thighs, and Johnny and I sat in two chairs across from him. The back of my chair felt stiff, unyielding.

"How is Mia?" I asked. I could still see Monique's shimmering blue dress, hear her lilting voice.

Mr. Greene's brow furrowed. "She's one lucky girl to have a neighbor like you."

Lucky that she'd lost her parents? "Have you figured out how the fire started?"

"We believe the fire was intentionally set." Mr. Greene betrayed no emotion, no bias. "We've ruled out all accidental causes."

"Damn," Johnny said, his face hard.

The words *intentionally set* ricocheted in my brain, and I struggled for breath for a moment. "Can you tell us anything more?"

Mr. Greene cleared his throat, looked down at his computer screen, and then at me again. "I can't disclose anything yet, but it's important that you tell me everything you remember about the night of the fire, even if it doesn't seem significant."

I glanced out the window at the twilight sky. What would Mr. Greene find important? Monique's tone of voice as she'd looked up the stairs and asked about Johnny? Adrian watching from Jessie's front porch? "The Kimballs came back a few days early. They were on vacation in Hawaii, on the Big Island."

He typed on his tablet. "What time was that?"

"Around dusk."

"Do you know why they came back early?"

"Monique said it was complicated. Something like that."

"Then what happened?"

"They had a barbecue in their backyard, and I went to bed. I heard a car prowling up the road, maybe around eleven. Then I fell asleep, and something woke me up. It was 1:17 a.m., I remember looking at my clock."

"Something woke you up?" His left eyebrow rose.

"I vaguely remember a loud sound. And smoke and flames coming from next door, on the first floor, and the Kimballs' fire alarm. I heard Mia crying."

Johnny remained silent, tense.

Mr. Greene kept tapping on his computer, then looked up at me again. His direct gaze unnerved me. "What color was the smoke? Black, gray, white? The flames?"

"The smoke was black, I think. But it was dark outside, hard to tell. The flames were bright orange."

"Did you notice anything else unusual before the fire? A dog barking? Anyone hanging around the neighborhood?"

I felt both men looking at me intently. "Monique came over to borrow charcoal. But it wasn't unusual. She's always borrowing things. *Was.*"

"Anything else?"

"We saw Jessie across the street, sitting on her porch with a boy. I think it was her boyfriend, Adrian. Her parents weren't home, but they came out later, during the fire."

Mr. Greene frowned as he tapped in more notes. He looked up at me again. "How do you know Jessie's parents weren't home earlier in the evening?"

"They drive a silver Honda. They always take that car when they go out. There was a black Buick in the driveway. Adrian drives a black Buick. Jessie wouldn't have him over if her parents were home. Do you think Jessie or Adrian set the fire?"

"Jessie's a good girl," Johnny said. "She would never do anything like that."

"You'd be surprised," Mr. Greene said.

"We know Jessie," I said. But did we? Did I know anyone on that street well enough to know if they would set a fire? Mr. Calassis? His wife, Maude? Chad and Monique? "Jessie took care of the house while the Kimballs were away. Picked up their mail and watered their plants. Monique mentioned something had gone missing this time. A gold pen. But she said it might have fallen behind the fridge."

Mr. Greene looked up at me again. "Did you see Jessie enter the Kimballs' house that day?"

"No, but I'm not always looking out my window."

"You said she had a key?"

I nodded. "Sometimes we don't bother to lock our doors. *Didn't.* Nothing ever happens there . . . usually."

"Any reason anyone would want to set fire to the Kimballs' house?"

Johnny frowned and shook his head. "No, none whatsoever."

"No," I echoed. "Why would anyone set fire to any house?"

Outside, the sky had turned inky black, devoid of stars.

"Did you ever hear the Kimballs fighting?" Mr. Greene asked. "Any sign of trouble?"

"Sometimes they raised their voices," I said. "All couples do that, don't they?"

"Did they raise their voices that night?"

"I didn't hear any arguments, no."

Mr. Greene gazed hard at me, as if trying to see into my brain. "Your window was open. You heard Mia crying, and you went outside . . ."

I told him everything that had happened next, everything I could remember. "The fire shot out Mia's window and jumped to our house."

"An open window can act as a chimney, sucking air in the bottom and shooting smoke from the top. Dry, windy night, embers flew . . ."

"And burned down our house. I broke Mia's window—"

"You had no other choice. You saved the little girl, don't forget." Mr. Greene gave me a sympathetic look, and I fought tears again.

"What about fraud?" Johnny said. "Could the Kimballs have hired someone to set fire to their own house?"

I gazed at him, speechless. How could that be possible?

Mr. Greene looked from Johnny to me and back. "Fraud is becoming more common these days. People want out—they're underwater on their mortgages, or they've lost their jobs, their businesses are failing—"

"Why would our neighbors *kill themselves*?" I said. I couldn't imagine Chad or Monique concocting such a scheme.

"Maybe they thought they could get out in time," Johnny said. "I'm not saying that's what happened, but . . ."

"Why would they leave Mia in her room?" I said sharply. "They wouldn't do that."

Mr. Greene raised a brow. "Never know. One thing I've learned in this profession. People do strange things, things you wouldn't believe."

"But the Kimballs would not put their own child in danger," I insisted. Or would they?

Mr. Greene looked at Johnny. "You were away at a medical conference?"

"Yes," Johnny said.

"In California?"

"San Francisco."

"When did you leave?"

"Two nights before the fire. I flew down—"

"And when did you fly back?"

"I was supposed to be there for two more days. When I got Sarah's message, I called her back, but Pedra Ramirez answered and told me Sarah was in the hospital. I flew back right away."

"On a red-eye?"

"Yes," Johnny said. "How is this relevant?"

My shoulders tensed.

"You weren't available to answer your wife's original call during the fire," Mr. Greene said.

Johnny looked at Mr. Greene with a touch of regret in his eyes. "I spoke to her earlier in the evening, but yes, I missed her second call."

"In the middle of the night." Mr. Greene stared at Johnny.

Johnny did not flinch. "My colleague had just lost a patient to cancer. We were down in the hotel bar."

"Commiserating?"

"You could say that."

"Female colleague, or male?"

"Female," Johnny said. "I didn't hear my phone. What does this have to do with the fire?"

Mild nausea rose in my throat, perhaps a side effect of the concussion. Johnny had told me the same story.

"Covering all the bases." Mr. Greene glanced at his watch, got up, and flipped the cover shut over the tablet computer. "Thanks. I'll be in touch."

I got up, too, and I must've been swaying a little, because Johnny wrapped his arm around my waist to steady me. "You okay? Need water?"

"I'm a little tired." I sat back in the chair as Johnny and Mr. Greene headed for the door.

"I appreciate your time," I heard Mr. Greene say in the foyer.

"No problem," Johnny said curtly. The front door creaked open and shut. I felt disoriented, my mind in a jumble. A fresh headache pressed at my temples. The fire wouldn't leave my brain—the odors of burning wood and chemicals, Mia's cries. The smoke. I thought of Mr. Greene's questions to Johnny, about his whereabouts the night of the fire. He wouldn't lie to me, never had. I trusted him more than I'd ever trusted anyone. He had been in the hotel bar, comforting a colleague, just as he'd told me. Besides, where else would he have gone?

CHAPTER SEVEN

Johnny loved to cook, but now every dog-eared cookbook, every note he'd made, every tomato stain on the pages had burned away. He'd made a quick shopping trip downtown, and on our first night in the cottage, he planned to try a Thai recipe from a new paperback he'd bought at the Shadow Cove Bookstore.

"I'm rebuilding our library, one step at a time," he said, opening to a peanut curry page. He laid out the ingredients on the counter. He'd had to buy new spices. Our extensive collection was gone—imported saffron, organic turmeric, sea salt. He hummed while he worked, his vain attempt at normalcy.

I came up behind him, wrapped my arms around his waist. I needed to feel his solidity, his familiar warmth. We needed to hang on to the rituals of everyday life. The sizzling curry smelled like home, like an evening the previous summer, when Johnny had marinated chicken for dinner with the Kimballs, curried tofu slices for me. The tofu hadn't been firm enough; it had crumbled and fallen through the barbecue grill. Monique had told me, *You need meat for your libido,* but as she'd spoken, she'd been looking at Johnny. What had she meant by that? Had she been suggesting that I couldn't give Johnny what he needed sexually? At the time, the comment had barely registered in my mind. Why had it resurfaced now?

"You don't need to cook," I said, squeezing Johnny around the waist. "We could've ordered takeout."

"I wanted to. I wish I could bring back our house, but all I can do is make food for you."

"Just be here with me. That's all I need. But I wish you hadn't accepted Eris's dinner invitation. I'd rather be a hermit."

"We don't have to go. I'll cancel."

"No, don't. She's been so kind to us—"

"We won't stay long, then." He turned off the stove, put the spatula on the counter.

"Promise."

"Cross my heart." He turned to face me, wrapped his arms around me. "I should've been there for you."

"It's not your fault. You couldn't have known what would happen."

"But I feel responsible."

"You're not."

He scooped me up, carried me down the hall and across the threshold into the tiny master bedroom, as if this was our honeymoon night.

"Hey, what about dinner?" I said as he laid me gently on the bed.

"Dinner can wait." He kissed me again, long and deep. I closed my eyes, and in my mind, the dim cottage bedroom expanded into our brightly lit suite on Sitka Lane. The ceiling became a glass skylight, revealing the brilliant constellations. Surely the heavens knew why two homes had burned down, why two people had died. In my imagination, I could undo the damage, resurrect the dead, turn darkness into light. Anything was possible.

Almost.

Somewhere in the distance, while Johnny and I made love, I heard his cell phone belting out a familiar, funky melody. He'd changed the ringtone again. The lyrics came to me as the song, by En Vogue, played over and over before the call kicked into voice mail: *Lies, lies . . . using lies as alibis.*

***

Later, we ate off hand-painted ceramic dishes that had come with the cottage. We squished in next to each other at the breakfast nook, so much smaller than our dining table on Sitka Lane, the one with a large extra leaf for guests. We'd bought the oak table on impulse, on sale; one leg had been slightly shorter than the others. The table had tilted and jiggled.

"I hope some of our furniture survived," I said to Johnny. After we'd made love, he had checked his voice mail, but he had not returned the call.

He took a deep breath. "The first time I went back there, the investigators were still checking for exposed wires, things like that. But we can go in now."

"Maybe tomorrow," I said.

"After work, okay? Wait for me."

I nodded, although a different plan began to form in my mind. After dinner, we cleaned up the kitchen in a silent, well-practiced duet. Johnny rinsed the plates and I dropped them into the dishwasher. In this smaller space, which forced us to nearly bump elbows, I became more aware of the ritual.

Then I faced the ordeal of unpacking, hanging my sparse belongings in the tiny bedroom closet. Had I been spoiled, lavish with my walk-in closet on Sitka Lane? Not that I'd sought luxury. The closet had already been there when I'd met Johnny—the shelves had been waiting to hold my favorite cotton pajamas, my soft jeans. Nobody had ever lived with him in that house, although I knew he'd been seriously involved with a woman once or twice. He remained vague about his past, sometimes brooding. It seemed his relationships had never lasted long, until he'd met me. *There's something about you, Sarah Phoenix,* he'd said after we'd been seeing each other for a few weeks. *Something permanent.*

I smiled at the memory. He'd wanted to move quickly, to become engaged after only a few months, but I'd been cautious, dating him nearly eighteen months before accepting his marriage proposal. His persistence had paid off.

But I had to admit, I missed the sweater Nana had knitted for my twenty-fifth birthday. I missed her portrait of Miracle Mouse. Had any part of the painting survived? I hadn't allowed myself to speculate. Another song played a soothing melody in my mind: *Que sera, sera. Whatever will be, will be.*

Johnny had deposited the gifts from the hospital in the second bedroom, where I'd propped the Wonder Woman card on his temporary desk. A few friends had called—authors in my writing group, a couple of Johnny's coworkers. The generosity warmed my heart as I sifted through a small bundle of greeting cards. *We're thinking of you. We're here for you.*

Near the bottom of the pile, I came across an unusual card. On the front, a cartoon clove of garlic roasted on a campfire, red-cheeked and wide-eyed, its mouth a jagged line of misery. The words at the top read, "Holy Toledo!" Inside, written in flamboyant script, were the words

Dear Dr. Johnny McDonald,

Try to think of this time as necessary preparation for wonderful things to come.

The squiggly signature was illegible.

Wonderful things? Necessary? Who would write such a thing?

I showed Johnny the card. He sat at the breakfast nook, checking email on his laptop computer.

"Who's it from?" he asked, peering closely at the signature inside the card.

"You can't tell?"

"Nope. But it's in bad taste. Why would a fire be preparation for anything wonderful?"

"My thoughts exactly." I felt a strange turning in my gut.

He ripped up the card and threw it in the recycling basket. "Forget about it now."

"Forgotten already." I kissed his cheek. "I'm going to run a bath."

"I'll join you in a bit," he said, not looking up from the computer.

I found lavender salts in the medicine cabinet and filled the tub. As I sank into the hot, soothing water, my hair floating to the surface, I thought of a warm Sunday afternoon the previous summer, when I'd been upstairs cleaning the window in our bedroom. I'd spotted Monique in her yard, floating nude on her back in Mia's plastic swimming pool. Johnny had been downstairs in his study, on the opposite side of the house. Had he seen her? Had she wanted someone to see her? Perhaps she hadn't even thought about her nakedness. But I had felt uncomfortable, like an unwilling voyeur—and somehow physically inadequate compared to the voluptuous, sensual French woman on the block.

Now, as I emerged from the bathwater, I heard Johnny speaking in a hushed tone in the master bedroom. I stepped out of the tub. Without pulling the plug from the drain, I dried my skin, wrapped myself in a towel, and tiptoed to the bathroom door, which I'd left ajar. Closed doors had always made me claustrophobic—even more so now. I could hear a little better from here, a few words drifting in now and then.

" . . . as long as it takes . . . She can't know . . ."

I backed up, pulled the plug, and the water began to drain noisily away. I hummed to myself as if everything was okay, which it was, wasn't it? My humming drowned out his voice, drowned out my own unsettling thoughts. Why had I eavesdropped? Sometimes Johnny lowered his voice if he received an important call in a public place. He was often on call for his clinic. But I'd never heard him speak in a hushed tone at home.

As the water finished draining from the tub, Johnny strode in and took me in his arms. "Damn, I'm too late. I thought I would take a bath with you."

"I heard you talking to someone." I looked in the mirror, still foggy around the edges.

After a barely perceptible hesitation, he said, "Yeah. Work." He stood behind me and caressed my shoulders.

"You said 'as long as it takes.' And 'she can't know.'"

"You heard all that?" His brows rose.

"It almost sounded as if . . ."

"As if what?" The fog began to clear from the mirror.

"I thought you might be talking about me, trying to keep something from me."

"From *you?*" He laughed. "Hell no. A patient called about his dermabrasion treatments. He doesn't want his wife to know."

"He's embarrassed?"

"You could say that."

"Poor guy." I ran a comb through my wet hair.

"Do you often eavesdrop on my calls?"

"No," I said. "It was just . . ." What?

His hands dropped from my shoulders. "I wasn't talking about you." Did his eyes darken in the mirror?

"I know you weren't. Let's start over. We could still take a bath. I could refill the tub, add some bubbles."

But he was already turning to leave the room.

CHAPTER EIGHT

Johnny fell asleep easily, while I lay awake, every sound magnified—the whirr of the heater, creaks as the cottage settled, Johnny's steady breathing. The wind whipped through the fir branches, and somewhere in the distance, a great horned owl hooted. The owl would've delighted Monique. Felix Calassis had inspired her interest in birds. She had once explained the words for owl in French. An owl with tufted ears was *une chouette*, while the general word for owl was *un hibou*. Her lips had puckered provocatively when she'd pronounced the words. Everything about her had simmered with sexuality, even her voice when she'd sung while working in the garden. *Parlez-moi d'amour. Speak to me of love.* I could see her, the way she'd sat on her heels, wiping her forehead with the back of her hand, staring into space. She'd slipped into reveries. What unspoken secrets had she taken with her to the grave? What unfulfilled dreams?

Eventually, I fell asleep and dreamed, too, of the house on Sitka Lane. A shaft of moonlight illuminated the familiar objects of home. We were happy and safe. Monique and Chad were okay. The fire, the deaths—it had all been a terrible misunderstanding.

I woke in darkness and remembered where I was, in the cottage on Shadow Bluff Lane. Home no longer existed. Chad and Monique were gone forever. Why did I keep forgetting? With the realization came a devastating sinking of my heart.

The faint smell of smoke wafted into my nose. The window was open, the curtain flapping against the screen. *Not again. This can't be happening.* My breathing grew shallow, my hands curled into fists. The clock radio read 2:00 a.m. in blocky blue numbers. I reached for Johnny but he was gone. My fingers slid across a wrinkled bedspread, an empty pillow. Where could he be at this hour?

I got up, pulled on my new robe and slippers. The cottage emitted unfamiliar smells—mildew and a hint of stale perfume. Strange shadows slithered across the room, and furniture shapes elongated, alive. Maybe the smoke was coming from a neighbor's house or from the forest. My heartbeat quickened. I broke out in a sweat. "Johnny!" I called. No answer.

In the living room, I found no sign of him. He wasn't anywhere in the cottage. He'd vaporized into thin air. I peered out the kitchen window, across the gently sloping garden, toward the street. Near Eris's house, a single streetlamp flickered, casting a triangle of feeble light. The odor of smoke came from somewhere across the road.

Johnny's car still sat in the driveway. He'd left his cell phone on the nightstand, but his rain jacket was missing from the hook beside the door, his running shoes gone from the mat.

I found a flashlight in a kitchen drawer, pulled on a sweatshirt and jeans, socks, and sneakers. Out on the porch, in the cool air, I swept the beam across the yard. Crickets clicked in the underbrush, and I could hear the distant rushing of the river. No sign of Johnny, and no response when I called his name.

The night wind swirled around me, prodding me with chilled fingers as I followed the flashlight beam down the driveway, along the road toward the white Victorian. As I climbed Eris's driveway, the flashlight beam dimmed. The house loomed ahead of me in silence, the windows black and ominous, a single beacon of light on the porch. If Johnny had come here, a light would be on inside the house. The smell of smoke receded behind me now, so I turned around and retraced my steps.

Had he gone into the woods? Out for a midnight run? Maybe he'd woken up and couldn't get back to sleep. When I was halfway back to the cottage, the flashlight battery died, leaving only a sliver of moonlight to show me the way. The odor of smoke still drifted through the air, earthy and woody, different from the caustic smell of the Kimballs' fire. I followed the gray curve of the road, and as I approached the driveway, a shadow moved on the porch.

"Johnny!" I called out. I tapped the flashlight, flicked the switch on and off. Nothing. "Johnny," I called out again. The shadow moved off the porch and into the woods. Had I imagined someone there?

I ran up the driveway, nearly tripping over my own feet, my heart pounding. I burst in through the front door, turned on the porch light with trembling fingers. The light spilled out across the grass. Nobody there.

"Johnny!" I called out again, my voice high-pitched. Eris's house remained dark, but on the other side, a light came on in the neighbors' window. I thought I heard voices carried on the wind. A figure advanced on the road, coming from the direction of the A-frame house. I should go back inside, I thought, and call 911, but then the figure waved at me.

"Sarah!"

It was Johnny.

Had he been at the neighbors' house? Visiting Theresa?

"Yeah, here!" I shouted back. I nearly collapsed with relief.

As he jogged up the driveway, entering the circle of light by the porch, I could see that he'd put on jeans and a T-shirt beneath his rain jacket. All while I'd been asleep. Usually, I was a light sleeper. He could wake me by sneezing or coughing. But he'd remained utterly silent, or I'd slept more deeply than usual. Perhaps the concussion had altered my brain chemistry.

I crossed my arms over my chest, my teeth chattering in the cold. "Where were you? What's going on? Where's the smoke coming from?"

"I went to investigate," he said, a little breathless. "What are you doing up?"

"I wondered where you were. Where's the fire?"

"Neighbors' house." He ran up the steps and hugged me, ushering me inside. "The smoke's coming from the fireplace, that's all."

"Did you talk to the neighbors?" The blood rushed loudly in my head.

"I saw the smoke coming from the chimney," he said. "That's all it is."

"At this hour?" I peered out the window at the light still shining through the trees.

"They must stay up late." As he brushed past me, a subtle, strange smell rose from him, the slight odor of a chemical similar to paint thinner. Then it was gone. The light in the A-frame house winked out, plunging the forest into darkness.

CHAPTER NINE

By the time I woke in the morning, Johnny had returned from his run. I sat at the breakfast nook in my pajamas while he made bagels and cream cheese. The neighborhood appeared safe, benign, the trees benevolent, wrens chattering in the underbrush. No smoke rose from the neighbors' chimney.

Johnny handed me a cup of coffee. The liquid in the mug looked darker than usual and tasted unusually sweet.

"It's the soy milk," he said. "I accidentally picked up vanilla instead of plain."

"It's great," I said. "I didn't hear you get up last night."

"You were in a deep sleep. Moaning and mumbling."

"No, I wasn't." I laughed.

"Snoring, too. Loud as a motor."

"I never snore. Maybe it's the concussion. I feel all right."

"Are you sure?" His brow furrowed, his expression shifting to concern.

"I'm sure." I looked down into the coffee, then up at him. "Did you talk to them?"

"To whom?" He made himself busy at the kitchen counter. He still wore his running shoes, Nike T-shirt, and Lycra exercise pants, which accentuated the muscles in his thighs.

"The neighbors. Last night."

He hesitated. "Nope. Just looked. Saw the smoke."

I sipped more sickly-sweet coffee. "How long had you been over there when I got up?"

"I dunno, a few minutes."

"I didn't hear you get dressed."

"I didn't want to wake you."

"You're so thoughtful," I said.

"You take me for granted."

"I know I do. You always make me breakfast."

"Because I love you only."

"Me, too. I love you only."

He came to me and gently kissed my forehead. "If you want the car today, you have to drive me to work."

"Oh yeah. I forgot." My smoke-damaged Camry was in the shop. I finished my coffee and rushed to the bedroom to get changed.

As I drove him downtown through a crisp, bright autumn day, a mild headache pushed at my temples. I tried to ignore the pain—the neurologist had warned me about the aftereffects of my injury. But how long would they last?

In the clinic parking lot, Johnny gave me a perfunctory peck on the cheek, not his usual kiss on the lips.

"Are you okay?" I asked, pulling back.

"It's going to be a hard day. Difficult cases."

"The dermabrasion guy?"

"That's an easy one."

I squeezed his arm.

He got out and strode briskly into the clinic. As he looked at his cell phone screen, I thought of an article Natalie had shown me, when she'd worried Dan might be having an affair.

Signs your husband is cheating:

He makes phone calls in private.

You notice a new scent on him.

He travels more for work.

His behavior changes.

Not the normal kiss good-bye.

Dan was faithful to Natalie, but I realized now that Johnny fit the pattern. He'd smelled different when we'd arrived at the cottage. He traveled more these days, wandered outside in the night, pecked me on the cheek.

Before my father had moved out, he'd been away more often and for longer periods of time. He'd come home carrying new soap smells from the cities he'd visited and gifts for me and my mother—perhaps to assuage his guilt. My mother had remained willfully oblivious until she could no longer ignore the evidence.

I'm never going to hurt you, Johnny had told me. *You can always trust me.* And I did. A peck on the cheek meant nothing. Neither did quiet calls while I was in the bath or a walk down the street at two a.m. I would not let my deadbeat father's affairs determine my attitude toward men for the rest of my life.

I drove out of the lot, stopped for supplies at the hardware store, then headed straight to Sitka Lane and parked at the curb. I sat in the driver's seat, unable to tear my gaze from the bombed-out war zone that had once been our home. But the headache had begun to recede, and I felt stronger today, determined to salvage anything I could from the ash.

Mr. Calassis came out onto his porch across the street, training his binoculars high in a fir tree. He suffered from the beginnings of dementia, his memory disappearing in thin slices. He spotted me and hurried across the street, his pants billowing in the breeze. As usual, his binoculars hung around his neck.

I got out of the car, a rush of warmth infusing me as he pulled me into a wordless hug, the binoculars bumping against my chest. He pulled away and patted my cheek. His sparse white hair was combed back, his face ruddy, and he smelled mildly of pipe tobacco. "Good to see you alive and kicking."

"Likewise."

He glanced toward the rubble and shook his head. "The fire was no accident."

"Arson, I know. Did you see anything?"

"Of course I did."

"What did you see?" The breeze grew colder on my face.

"Felix!" Maude Calassis stepped out on her porch. "We'll be late!"

"Coming!" He waved at her and frowned, then turned back to me. "You be careful now."

"Careful of what?"

He glanced toward the Kimballs' rubble again. "I always knew that woman was trouble."

"Who, Monique?" I said, but he was already heading for home. "Mr. Calassis?" But he didn't turn around. I ran after him and tugged at his sleeve.

He turned to look at me and smiled. "Sarah, glad to see you alive and kicking."

"You said I should be careful—about a woman?"

He didn't answer. His gaze shifted upward, familiar blankness in his eyes. I let go of his sleeve, my heart plummeting, and watched him shuffle home.

Back at the car, I put on the gloves, mask, and protective booties I'd bought at the hardware store, and I grabbed two large plastic bags. Taking a deep breath, I stepped through the space where the front door had stood. The foyer was unrecognizable. I could roughly tell where the hallway had been, as well as the outline of the living room and family room. Half a sink remained in the downstairs bathroom. Debris from the second floor had fallen through the ceiling.

Even through the mask, I could smell the burned fabric and plastic. As I picked my way across the rubble, my breathing grew loud in my ears. The ghosts of our past life drifted through me. The dining table was gone, and all the stuffing had burst out of the charred blue couch. But I uncovered a warped paperback copy of Daphne du Maurier's *Rebecca*, smoke damaged but intact.

In my study, I found no trace of the painting of Miracle Mouse, not even a scrap of canvas. But I discovered the useless remains of the monitor and printer; the computer hard drive had melted. How many days had I spent in here, writing? I could see the room as it had once been, awash in afternoon sunlight.

In Johnny's office, three jagged walls still stood. I kneeled to brush away ash, picked up various recognizable objects—stapler, flashlight, pens—before I glimpsed the edge of an envelope sticking out from beneath a warped metal shelf.

I retrieved the envelope and pulled out a set of singed photographs depicting rivers, beaches, Mount Rainier—and one of Johnny sitting on a dock in swimming trunks, dangling his feet in a lake, a forest in the background. A ramshackle fisherman's hut rose from the dock, the glass missing from its windows. A woman sat next to Johnny, her bare, tanned shoulder touching his, the picture ending at the black strap of her bikini.

Johnny's blue Speedo swimming trunks looked familiar. He'd owned them before I'd met him. He'd worn them several times since. In the picture, he looked muscular, his hair windswept, the way it was now. He didn't look any younger than he did today, but then, the picture had been taken from a distance. The fine lines on his face were not discernible. On the back of the photo, someone had handwritten in beautiful script, *For Johnny, my love.*

For a moment, I stopped breathing. The words reached up and slapped me in the face. The photograph had been taken before I'd met him. Had to have been. He'd been in love before, so what? Or at least, a woman had loved *him.* But of course. Johnny was irresistibly masculine, if not classically handsome. And he was smart, and loving, and thoughtful. What woman wouldn't want him? He had a past, so what? What did I expect?

I found many things I couldn't remember ever seeing—a pair of reading glasses, a designer pen, a silver bracelet. In the remains of other rooms, I picked up more charred objects—a cup; a hand-painted, cracked ceramic bowl; a gold necklace. But no more photographs.

Finally, exhausted, I returned to the car and stowed the bags in the back. As I closed the trunk, Pedra Ramirez burst out of her house and scurried down her driveway in a red linen shirt, khaki Capris, and bright red sandals. She hurried across the road. "Sarah! *Díos mio.* You're never going to believe what's happened."

CHAPTER TEN

Pedra rushed up and hugged me, exuding her characteristic gardenia scent. *"Lo que es una tragedia."* She shook her head, her hoop earrings glinting in the sunlight. "First the fire, and now . . ."

"Now what? What's going on?"

"It's Mia," Jessie shouted, racing outside in bare feet. She threw herself at me with abandon, embracing me in a tight, desperate hug, giving off smells of lemon shampoo and bubble gum. Her eyes were rimmed with black kohl.

"What about Mia?" I said, pulling away. "Is she okay?"

"I called her grandma," Pedra said. "You know, to see how they're doing."

"She got hold of the scissors," Jessie said.

"She what? Is she hurt?" I thought of all the hazards in a home that could harm a vulnerable child.

"She cut off her hair," Jessie said.

"Kids sometimes do that," I said.

Pedra shook her head. "But her grandma, she is too old. She doesn't pay attention, or she falls asleep."

"We're worried," Jessie said. "We're about to go over there—"

"I'll go," I said. "Where do they live?"

"Ferndale Glen. I can give you the address." Jessie copied the address from her cell phone to mine. Her dangling copper leaf earrings shone in the light. Something nagged at me about her, but I couldn't figure out what.

"Don't say I told you," she said, stepping away from me and biting her lip. "You know, about her hair."

"Don't worry," I said. "My lips are sealed."

As I drove up the road, I passed Adrian's black Buick on its way to Jessie's house. Had I heard his car that night? Impossible to know for sure. As we passed each other, he looked at me through his open window. He was powerfully built, his long hair tied back. His eyes were devoid of expression. Almost creepy. I pressed the accelerator, hit the speaker button on my cell phone and the speed dial for Johnny. He answered almost immediately. "Tough day here. You caught me between appointments."

"I'm on my way to see Mia. She cut off her hair. Pedra told me."

Johnny's voice sharpened. "You went by the house without me?"

"I found a picture of you with an old girlfriend. Sitting on a dock at a lake. There's an old building on the dock. Who's the woman?"

"I would have to see the picture. There were so many women." He seemed to think this was banter.

"I thought I knew everything about you." But I had to admit, I'd held on to a few pictures of old boyfriends, too. At least, before the fire.

"Does anyone ever know everything about anyone else?"

"Is that a tongue twister?"

"You've still got a lot to learn about me and vice versa. I'll tell you anything you need to know."

"Anything?"

"Ask away, and I'll answer. I used to wear boxers before I switched to tighty-whities. I have nothing to hide, except . . . well, maybe a few small things."

"Like what?" My heartbeat sped up.

"Like, I had acne when I was twelve. Gigantic cysts. That's the real reason I became a dermatologist."

"You're making this up."

"You're right. The truth is, my grandfather died of melanoma."

"I'm so sorry. Why didn't you tell me?" I knew his grandfather had died in his fifties, but I hadn't known how. What else was Johnny keeping from me?

"I didn't want to talk about it. I wish I could've saved him."

"Now you're spending your life making up for it, trying to save others."

"Something like that."

"You're doing a great job. Oh, I'm almost here. Gotta go."

I hung up as I turned onto Ferndale Glen and parked in front of Harriet Kimball's house, a pink bungalow with a double garage and thick lace curtains in the windows. Well-tended, dormant rosebushes dotted the front garden, waiting for the sun to return in spring.

I strode up the driveway and knocked on Harriet's front door. When she answered, she looked as if she had worked hard to unwind her years. Her face appeared smooth but not young, as if she'd ironed every wrinkle into submission. A layer of powdered foundation covered her cheeks. She wore the same auburn wig that I remembered from her visits to Sitka Lane. Only now it was clear that the wig was actually her own hair, growing from her very own scalp. Her eyes were red-rimmed and puffy.

"Sarah," she said in a throaty voice.

"I'm so sorry . . ."

Harriet's lips trembled, and she wiped away tears, smearing her makeup. "I'm sorry, too. Sorry about your home. I can't thank you enough for saving Mia."

"I wish I could've done more." My skin felt thin, my insides vulnerable. Without thinking, I pulled Harriet into a tight hug, surprised at the woman's frailty. How cruel life could be, how senseless. A son wasn't supposed to leave his elderly mother with only her memories and a grandchild to care for alone.

"You did more than enough." Harriet ushered me inside, closed the door, and pressed a finger to her lips. "She's asleep," she said softly.

I mouthed "Oh" and looked around at the comfortable furniture, everything lived-in, plush. Harriet's home reflected her love for roses—rose-print couch, rose-colored chair, plastic roses in a vase. Dolls, picture books, and balled-up tissues were strewn here and there among the roses.

"She hasn't slept well," Harriet said, walking stiffly to the couch. She sat down just as stiffly.

I remained standing at the threshold of the living room. The air smelled faintly of rosewater and Nivea cream. I glanced down the dim hallway to the left and imagined Mia crying for her parents, cutting off her hair while Harriet slept. "Can I see her now?"

"Maybe when she wakes up." Harriet gestured to a chair. "Want to sit? I should've offered you tea."

I removed my shoes and padded to the chair in my socks, not wanting to smudge dirt on the pale pink carpet, although faint stains marred its original luster.

I sat in a worn armchair. "Is Mia okay? Are you okay?"

"We're getting by."

Across the room, a tall bookshelf held an assortment of novels, including a set of Miracle Mouse mysteries. As Harriet got up unsteadily and shuffled toward the bookshelf, she looked for a moment like Nana. My throat tightened, tears springing to my eyes. In her last days, illness had reduced my grandmother from a strong, outspoken artist to a quiet, brittle shell. Until now, I'd always had the portrait of Miracle Mouse to remind me of Nana in her better days.

When Harriet bent to retrieve an old photo album from the bottom shelf, the resemblance disappeared. Her hair was too dark, her shoulders too narrow. She sat on the couch again, patted the cushion next to her. I went over to sit with her.

"I had framed photos all over the house," she said in a tremulous voice. "But I put them away. Chad is in nearly all of them. I feel like I'm betraying my little boy. But I can't bear to look at them." She took a crumpled tissue from her sweater pocket and wiped more tears from her cheeks.

Somewhere, a clock ticked away the hour. "I'm sure he would understand. We don't have to look at pictures—"

"I'm feeling a little brave, now that you're here." Harriet's fingers shook as she opened the album and pointed to a page-sized photo of a sleeping baby swaddled in soft blankets. "That's my boy," she whispered.

"He's beautiful," I replied. *Was.* How could she bear to look at her infant son?

"Always was." As she turned the pages, Chad grew from a chubby, blond toddler into a robust, sandy-haired boy. But Mia didn't look much like him. By early adolescence, he had acquired the husky body shape of a budding football player. Mia took after her delicate mother.

Harriet closed the album and heaved a sigh. Were her hands trembling from grief alone, or was it something else, too?

"Those are lovely pictures," I said. "Mia must miss her mom and dad."

Something hardened in Harriet's face. "Her mom. Chad fell head over heels in love with that woman. Nothing I could do to stop him. At least I have Mia. That's a blessing."

"May I see her now?" I said.

"All right, but she's done something naughty."

"Oh no, what?" I feigned surprise.

"You'll see. Come on." Harriet beckoned me down the hall and pointed into an untidy bedroom, all painted blue. The room must've once belonged to Chad. Mia's dolls and books and stuffed animals stood in stark contrast to the *Dukes of Hazzard* and *Star Wars* posters still plastered all over the walls. A worn desk and chest of drawers carried the nicks and battle scars of time.

Mia slept on a small bed by the window, splayed out on her back. Her chest rose and fell in an uneasy rhythm, her cheeks slightly flushed. She wore patched jeans and a pink T-shirt. A psychotic stylist had slashed at her golden locks, cutting at random. Her bangs fell in a jagged line.

"She got the scissors out of the drawer," Harriet whispered. "Children can be quick when you're not looking."

I tiptoed into the room. As I approached Mia, the little girl sighed and shifted. In sleep, she bore an even more remarkable resemblance to Monique. Streamlined nose with a slight rise at the tip, a smattering of translucent freckles, delicate jawline.

I sat next to Mia and kissed her cheek. She smelled like baby powder. She took a deep breath but didn't wake up. Her forehead felt cool and slightly damp to the touch. Since she'd cut her bangs, more of her scalp was visible. She did not appear to have any recent injuries—no bruises or wounds on her skin. A white scar sat up near the hairline, perhaps a healed cut or a birthmark similar to Johnny's. Her eyelids fluttered open. She sat up, dazed, and threw her arms around my neck. She said something quiet, something muffled.

"What is it, sweetie?" I said.

Mia repeated the word, louder this time. "Mommy."

CHAPTER ELEVEN

"You could adopt Mia," Natalie said on the phone as I drove back to the cottage. "Get the wheels turning before Grandma kicks the bucket."

"Natalie! Harriet loves Mia. She's her only living relative. They need each other."

"How old is that lady? Ninety-five?"

"Closer to eighty, I think."

"The average life expectancy for a woman in America topped out at eighty-six last year."

"You're a bottomless well of important facts." I turned onto Cedar Drive, which led to Shadow Bluff Lane. "We can't adopt Mia, Nat. We're homeless. I still have headaches. And I'm jumpy. Not my usual self."

"Your reactions are understandable. Just because you had some bad luck doesn't mean you would be a bad mother."

"When Mia realized I wasn't her mom, she started bawling." I'd rocked her, humming "Bright Morning Stars," the song my own mother had sung to me long ago. *Where are our dear mothers? They've gone to Heaven shouting* . . . Mia had quieted a little, but she could not be easily consoled.

"What are you going to do?"

"Harriet has to go into the hospital for some tests on Friday. She wants me to watch Mia for a few hours."

"Tests for what?"

"She mentioned 'remission' and feeling like whatever it is has returned."

"She has the big C? What did I tell you?"

"Natalie."

"There is no right answer. Follow your heart."

I hung up feeling oddly unmoored. Natalie had always been spontaneous, following her heart, while I weighed the pros and cons of every decision. She and Dan had fallen in love on their first date, while I'd been cautious with Johnny. I collected coupons, while she threw them into the recycling bin. She cooked elaborate meals, making huge messes, while I prepared simple dishes, cleaning up as I went along. If I wasn't writing late into the night.

At least, before the fire.

When I arrived at the cottage, a blue truck sat in the driveway, a Toyota Tundra, the logo on the side printed in bold yellow letters: Severson Home Repair and Remodeling. A tall, wiry man stood on the porch in a tool belt, work boots, a crisp white T-shirt, and a baseball cap.

"Can I help you?" I said, walking up to him.

"Todd Severson. I'm here to fix the flush and the living room window latch." His eyes looked slightly bloodshot, dark rings beneath them, as if he hadn't slept in days.

"The latch is broken?"

"Yeah. Ms. Coghlan sent me."

Could that be true? Would Eris have sent a man who looked so strung out? But he was suitably dressed, and he carried the proper tools. "She didn't tell me you were coming."

"I apologize for the intrusion, ma'am," he said, stepping back. He looped his left thumb over the top of his belt, like a cowboy. "I'll come back another time." He turned to leave.

"No, wait. I'll call her to make sure."

He nodded, tipping his baseball cap. I recognized him now, recognized the truck. I'd seen him around town, here and there, then again in Eris's driveway, when Johnny and I had moved into the cottage.

Eris answered after the first ring, and when I said "handyman," she gushed with apologies. "I should've called you first. I'll be over in a bit."

"You don't have to come," I said. "I just needed to be sure—"

"Not another word. And yes, I did hire him."

"Okay, good." I hung up and ushered him inside. "Sorry."

"No problem, ma'am." Mr. Severson stepped past me into the house. He emitted a faint whiff of some unusual herb, maybe sage. He gave me a penetrating, almost worried look, frown marks creasing the center of his forehead. Then he smiled, revealing slightly yellowed teeth, one chipped incisor, a dimple in his right cheek. He reached out a grimy hand to shake mine, then withdrew his hand quickly, seeming to notice for the first time that it was dirty. "Just came from another job." He wiped both hands down the thighs of his jeans.

"That's all right," I said, resisting the urge to wipe my hands, too.

"You're the new renter, then."

"My husband and I are," I said, hyperaware that I was alone in the house with a strange man.

Mr. Severson nodded again, his gaze traveling down across my body. Since the fire, none of my new clothes fit exactly right. "Wanna show me the faulty window?" he said. He had close-set eyes of indeterminate color, perhaps dark gray or brown.

"I didn't know there was a faulty window," I said.

"She said it was back here." He strode through the living room, jiggled the back window, then opened and shut it. "Latch doesn't work. See?"

I followed him. "I didn't realize. She didn't say."

"Dangerous in these times." He opened his toolbox and began to work on the latch with a wrench.

"It's pretty safe here, isn't it?" But then, I'd thought Sitka Lane was safe, too.

"We get break-ins now and then."

"On this street?"

"Don't know about this street. I got motion sensor lights out at my house. Did it for my wife, when she was living there."

"She's not there now?"

"She moved out a year ago. She was there when I went to work, gone when I got home. Just like that. Packed a bag and left me."

"I'm so sorry."

"We were married nine years. Coming on our anniversary. She took up with some carpenter in Bellingham. She broke my heart. My heart would still be broke, if I'd let it. But I moved on. You gotta move on, right?"

"Yes, you do," I said, not knowing what else to say. Although I had seen this man around town, the truth was, I didn't know him at all. Shadow Cove was big enough to allow anonymity, but small enough for the post office and grocery store clerks to recognize familiar faces, to allow the same people to cross paths more than once.

"Life. Gets you one way or another." He tried the window again. This time, the latch worked. "Good as new, if nobody don't throw a rock."

"Thank you," I said.

"No problemo." He looked out toward the woods, but he wasn't looking at the trees. He was looking past them, at something invisible. Then his eyes cleared and he looked at me. "Flush?"

"Down the hall. Hang on, let me make sure it's decent in there."

"I don't care about decent."

"But I do." I felt silly rushing ahead of him, but I managed to hide a bra beneath a towel before ushering him inside.

I stood in the doorway while he removed the lid from the toilet tank, stuck his hands in the water, and played with the flush contraption.

"Needs a new intake valve," he said.

"I have no idea what that is."

"Lucky for you, I do. Might have an extra one in the truck." He left and came back with a package and set to work on the toilet. "You should get motion sensor lights, too. On account of the break-ins."

"Well, we don't have anything to steal," I said. "Our house burned down. This is all we have."

"Sorry to hear that." He straightened and looked at me again, a spark of recognition in his eyes. "You the one . . . ?"

"I'm Sarah. Sarah Phoenix."

"I'll be damned," he said under his breath. His mouth dropped open, and he tottered a little, almost as if the utterance of my name had pushed him backward. He recovered quickly. "Sarah Phoenix, huh? The writer?"

"You've heard of me?"

"You and your husband, the skin doctor."

"Yes. How did you know?"

"I was there." As he spoke, a cloud crossed over the sun, plunging the room into shadow. Todd Severson's face darkened, the hollows and angles becoming more pronounced.

"What do you mean, you were there?" Ripples of apprehension traveled up my spine.

"I mean, I'm a volunteer firefighter for the seventh station."

"Oh." I exhaled. "Wow."

"Yeah." He closed the toilet tank and we stepped out into the hall. He looked at me in a different way now, with sadness in his eyes. "Ms.

Coghlan didn't tell me it was you. That you were renting this place, I mean. She just mentioned renters. Damn."

"You were on Sitka Lane that night. Which means you saw what happened, after I went to the . . . hospital."

He looked at the floor, then up at me again. "My unit was called out last. Volunteer station. We're close to Sitka Lane but we're not staffed twenty-four seven. Budget cuts and all. The central station was staffed. They went out first, but they're a ways off."

"But you did get there eventually," I said.

"Yeah, eventually," he said with deep regret. "But your neighbors . . . Damn."

"It wasn't your fault." I tried to picture Todd Severson in a fire-fighter's uniform.

"Nobody should've died," he said, shaking his head.

A black SUV rumbled up the road and parked at the curb. We both looked out the window, then Mr. Severson reached out to rest a hand on my shoulder. "If you need anything . . . If you have anything that you want help with . . ."

"We're okay. Thanks."

His eyes searched mine. "I'm sorry about what happened."

"Thank you," I said awkwardly.

"You need to be careful. That night . . ."

His cell phone rang in his back pocket. His mouth worked, as if he tasted something sour. "I got another job. Good to meet you, Sarah Phoenix." He strode to the front door before I could stop him and ask what he had been about to say. He stepped outside as Eris emerged from her SUV in an elegant, beige silk pantsuit and matching pumps. She hurried up the driveway. "Todd! Sarah!"

"Ma'am," Todd said, walking to his truck.

I stepped out as Eris strutted up the walkway in heels. "Todd! Is the flush fixed?"

"Right as rain," he said, opening the driver's side door.

"Bravo. The window?"

"Fixed."

"You're a lifesaver," she said.

"I'll bill you." He tipped his hat at me. "Good afternoon, ma'am."

"Thank you," I said.

He nodded and climbed into the truck. Eris and I watched as he backed out of the driveway and drove away.

Eris strode up to me, her heels clicking on the concrete. "How are you today? Did you go back to Sitka Lane?"

"I did. It was . . . difficult. I thought I would be able to salvage more of our belongings, but . . ."

"I'm so sorry," Eris said, her eyes full of sympathy.

"It's weird to know our home is open to the world. There's no front door. If there's anything left in that rubble, a thief could pick it up."

"That reminds me, I'll have Todd change the locks as well. He shouldn't have his own key to the cottage, but he's reliable, and the place was empty for so long—"

"I understand. I don't want to put you out."

"This is entirely my fault. We're still on for dinner? No need to bring anything."

"We both go to bed early—"

"I'm not surprised. I saw your husband out jogging at the crack of dawn when I was out for my hike. I didn't know he and Theresa knew each other. They were deep in conversation."

"Maybe he does," I said. I looked through the trees toward the A-frame house. I began to wonder exactly *how* Johnny knew Theresa. But why should I wonder? He knew so many people in Shadow Cove.

Eris followed my gaze. "You'll enjoy meeting her husband. Kadin is quite a handsome man."

"I'm sure he is. But, I've already got a handsome man of my own."

"Of course you do. Nobody could hold a candle to your husband, right?" She winked at me.

"Nobody in my universe," I said.

"But that Kadin . . . Ah well, he's taken, and I'm in a relationship." Eris sighed, glanced at her gold watch, then grinned at me. "Gotta run. Monthly meeting of the County Realtors Association. Dinner at my place at seven?"

"Thank you," I said, watching the A-frame again as Eris hurried back to her SUV and drove away.

CHAPTER TWELVE

At seven o'clock that evening, Johnny stood next to me on Eris Coghlan's front porch, still in his blue suit. Tucked under his arm: a bottle of expensive Chardonnay. After I'd picked him up from work, he'd taken so long to choose the right vintage at the wine shop, he'd barely had time to straighten his hair in the cottage. He'd glanced at the photo I'd found, but he couldn't remember who the woman was or where they had been.

I'd jokingly called him a player, unable to keep track of his dozens of past girlfriends. *I'm not like your father,* he'd said for the millionth time. He'd taken me in his arms, and we'd said no more about it.

Now, as we waited for Eris to answer the door, I could almost believe our lives were normal, that we were on one of our casual social outings. I'd donned dark jeans, a brown knit sweater, and Rockports. Everything new, except the gold necklace I'd found in the rubble, which I wore beneath the sweater, where nobody could see it—a reminder of my past life.

"Wish I'd had time to change," Johnny said, looking down at his suit.

"You went on an epic quest for the world's best Chardonnay." I slipped my hand into his.

"A joint quest with the world's most beautiful woman." He gazed down at me with that charming grin.

"You know the right things to say." I smiled at his words, although I was sure, with the stitches in my forehead, that I resembled a female version of Frankenstein's monster. At least the scar sat up near the hairline.

The door swung open, revealing Eris in a little black dress and heels. The fabric shone like freshly spun silk. She had the athletic build of a woman who worked out diligently, the muscles delineated on her arms. Suddenly, I felt horribly underdressed, frumpy, and out of shape. But I had nothing fancy to wear.

Eris broke into a warm smile and ushered us inside. The decorative wainscoting, high ceilings, and intricately carved crown moldings nearly made me gasp in admiration. I felt instantly homesick. "I'm so glad you could make it," Eris said, closing the door after us. The mouthwatering scents of garlic and onion wafted through the air, reminding me that I was famished.

A soft Brandenburg concerto drifted from another room. Eris looked at my shoes. "I'm a fan of Rockports. I'm a big sweater person, too."

I smiled, feeling a little more comfortable. "I'm slowly rebuilding my wardrobe."

"You're ahead of the game." She turned her smile to Johnny. "Wine! You shouldn't have."

He handed her the bottle. "Woodward Canyon, 2009, best Washington State Chardonnay ever."

"You didn't need to bring anything, but it's much appreciated."

Johnny flashed his disarming smile. "Least we could do."

"Dinner is a little late," she went on, as Johnny and I removed our shoes. "The lasagna needs a few more minutes. I got held up showing a spectacular home in Port Blakely, designed by Theo LaRoche."

Johnny's brows rose. "LaRoche. Talented guy."

"You've heard of him. I'm impressed."

I wasn't familiar with Theo LaRoche. Now I felt frumpy and uninformed, as well.

Eris tucked her hair behind her ear, revealing a teardrop pearl earring. "The house is right off Rockaway, stunning views of Blakely Harbor. Modern architecture. Big windows. Pennsylvania blue stone—"

"I love Pennsylvania blue," Johnny said.

"You do?" I said. This was news to me.

"Always have." His gaze remained focused on Eris.

All right, no problem. A wife could always learn something new about her husband, couldn't she?

"This one's going to go fast," Eris said. "I know of many other listings that might interest you."

"We plan to rebuild our house," I said.

Eris grinned at me. "Give me a chance. That's all I'm asking."

"No harm in looking," Johnny said. "Is there?" He squeezed my arm.

"All right, maybe a look," I said. It couldn't hurt, could it? I had dared to imagine Mia moving in with us. Maybe the little girl would do better away from reminders of her parents. No, that was a crazy thought. Mia belonged with her grandmother.

"Good, then. We'll make a date." Eris steered us into a spacious living room in which the Minkowskis already sat—Theresa, her fecund beauty filling the room, and her husband, who resembled a young Harrison Ford. They both stood, wineglasses in hand. Theresa wore a hip-hugging turquoise dress, her husband a pale green button-down shirt and black slacks. I was the only casually dressed person in the room.

"Kadin Minkowski," the man said, reaching out to shake Johnny's hand. "You've met Theresa."

Johnny smiled. "She came by the cottage. I'm Johnny McDonald, and this is my wife, Sarah."

"Pleasure." Kadin shook my hand next, his grip strong, on the edge of painful. Then he let go and stepped back, wrapping his arm around his wife's waist. "I was supposed to be out of town, but my meeting in LA was canceled at the last minute. Glad I have the chance to meet you instead."

I nodded and smiled. "So are we."

"Nice knowing the cottage is occupied," Theresa said. "We finally have neighbors."

Eris clapped her hands and said, "Well, now you're all better acquainted. Sarah and Johnny, raspberry wine?"

We both nodded, and she disappeared down the hall.

Theresa and Kadin sat next to each other on the only couch, more akin to a loveseat. Theresa sat at the edge. Johnny and I chose separate armchairs across from them. The room was furnished with heavy antique tables, bookshelves packed with old hardcovers, a crystal chandelier, Tiffany-style floor lamps.

Eris returned with two wineglasses for us. She sat in a high-backed Victorian armchair. "Johnny is a dermatologist, and Sarah writes children's books. Kadin is an investment manager, and Theresa is in restoration. Did I miss anyone?"

"Restoration?" Johnny said, looking at Theresa. "What's your specialty?"

Theresa crossed and uncrossed her shapely legs. "Fine arts. I'm restoring a Turkish decanter. The spout broke off. Now it's almost as good as new. You can't see the seams."

Johnny smiled appreciatively. "You perform magic."

She laughed. "We can't fix everything."

"Who can? It's hard when we're expected to perform miracles." Johnny and Theresa traded a look, some unspoken message passing between them.

"Readers expect perfection, as well," I said.

"You're writing a book, then?" Kadin said with interest.

"I'm supposed to be writing, yes, but it's a little difficult right now—"

"Did you always know?" Theresa cut in. "That you wanted to be a writer, I mean? Some people start writing when they're older, after they retire or raise their kids."

"I loved writing as a child, yes," I said. "But I didn't return to it until much later. I got a degree in psychology, thought I would go into research, but I became a reporter for the campus newspaper. I interviewed a cartoonist—and he reminded me of how much I'd loved writing when I was young."

"So you returned to it," Theresa said, smiling warmly. "How wonderful."

"Our son likes to write," Kadin said.

"Kadin Junior," Theresa said. "He just turned eight. He plays and runs like other kids, but the writing thing . . . We can't stop him. He uses his little computer, taps away—"

"He'll be a famous author someday," Kadin said, as if such a thing were easy to do. "He's got the keyboard fingers."

"And white patches on his arms," Theresa said, looking at Johnny. Here it came, the casting of a line to reel in free medical advice. "Any idea what that might be?"

Only I could detect the tightening of Johnny's fingers on the wineglass. "Hard to say without seeing him," he said. "Could be eczema or a superficial yeast infection."

"A yeast infection!" Kadin said. "I thought only women got yeast infections."

Theresa gave him a scolding look. "Kadin."

"Sorry. Couldn't help it."

"Could be psoriasis, vitiligo . . . ," Johnny went on.

"You mean what Michael Jackson had?" Kadin said.

"It's uncommon," Johnny said. "I would have to see your son. We can try to fit you in this week."

"He's the *best*," Eris cut in. "A miracle worker."

Johnny blushed. "I wouldn't say that."

"He cured *me*." Eris pointed to her cheek.

Theresa leaned in and squinted at Eris's cheek. "Cured you of what?"

"Exactly. It's gone," Eris said triumphantly.

Theresa sat back. "What was it? A minuscule pimple?"

"Melanoma," she said.

I remained quiet, a bit shell-shocked. Johnny had not told me that he already knew Eris, as well. I thought he'd met her through Maude.

Theresa gasped. "You had *skin cancer*?"

Eris touched her nose lightly. "Also here. My internist, who shall not be named, gave me a death sentence. He said I had six months to live."

"Six *months*?" Theresa's voice rose. "I had no idea."

Eris patted her arm. "Now you know. Dr. McDonald cured me. So far, no recurrence. We've had a couple of follow-ups."

Johnny fell silent, looking into his wine. He wouldn't divulge any privileged information about a patient, even if she revealed the information herself. But he could have told *me*. I was his wife, after all, and didn't husbands share secrets with their wives?

Theresa gave him an open look of admiration. "I'm glad to know a medical magician lives so close." She leaned forward to put her glass on the table, revealing ample cleavage.

Johnny smiled. "We can't fix everyone."

"Touché," Theresa said.

Tears came to Eris's eyes. "You gave me a whole new lease on life. The least I could do to return the favor is give you a place to live for as long as you need it."

It dawned on me then that Eris was not charging rent for the cottage. She meant to be generous, but I couldn't help feeling like an outsider, and I didn't want pity or charity.

When Eris called us all into the grand dining room for dinner, I barely tasted the spinach lasagna, despite my hunger. I wanted to run back to the cottage and hide. The laughter grated on me, the conversation trivial. Halfway through the meal, the doorbell rang, a melodic *ding-dong* reverberating through the house.

Eris dabbed at her mouth with a cloth napkin, slid her chair back, and stood. "Excuse me. I don't know who that could be this late."

Her pumps tapped the floor as she left the room. Everyone fell into uncomfortable silence as her voice drifted in, the rumble of a lower, male voice, then Eris's surprised laughter. "You're in luck! She's here. Come on in."

Eris returned to the dining room with a man in tow—bearded and slightly plump, he appeared to be in his thirties, in a yellow button-down shirt and blue jeans. Stitched into the shirt pocket was a badge reading *Harborside Florist*. He held a crumpled invoice in his hand. He looked a bit bewildered as he took in the dinner party, the well-dressed guests (all except me), the elaborate meal.

"Sorry to interrupt," he said, clearing his throat. "Delivery for Theresa Minkowski?" He looked at me.

"Not me," I said, smiling.

Theresa put her fork on her plate and looked up at him. "That's me. I'm Theresa." She glanced sidelong at Kadin. He betrayed no emotion.

The deliveryman shifted his gaze to Theresa. "I had the wrong address. Looks like a seven at the end. Should've been a one. I drove all around looking for two twenty-seven."

"We're two twenty-one," Theresa said.

The man sighed with visible relief. "I'll be right in with your delivery. I'm running late today. Looks like the order was placed this—"

"Please do bring them in," Eris said, sweeping her arms around the room expansively. "We're all curious."

The man returned a minute later carrying a spectacular, living turquoise hydrangea plant in a red ceramic pot. A small envelope was attached to a stick, propped in the soil.

The man looked around. "Where should I . . . ?"

"Why not right on the table?" Eris said, and grinned at Theresa. "What's the special occasion?"

"I'm not sure," Theresa said, but she was beaming.

As the man placed the pot on the table in front of Theresa, she stared at the hydrangea with delight.

"They're beautiful," I said, recalling the whole hedge of hydrangea plants in the backyard on Sitka Lane. Gifts from Johnny.

He sat motionless now, watching the scene unfold.

"Thank you very much," Theresa said to the deliveryman, who stood awkwardly in the arched entryway to the dining room.

"You're welcome," he said, tipping an imaginary hat. "Have a wonderful evening. I apologize for the interruption." He left in a hurry.

Eris sat, and we were all silent a moment, admiring the blooms. "Aren't you going to read the card?" she said.

Theresa reached for the card. We all watched her intently. She looked at Kadin and smiled. "You shouldn't have."

He grinned, but the grin did not reach his eyes. "They must be from your secret admirer."

"I don't have any secret admirers, except you." She turned the envelope around in her hands.

"Of course you do!" Eris said. "Open the card. You don't have to tell us what it says."

"I don't mind," Theresa said. She opened the card and read it in silence, then she smiled. "It says, *To an incredibly talented woman. A token of my appreciation for you only, and only you.*"

I froze, the words sharp, hanging in my mind like stalactites in an ice cave. Could more than one couple in the world share the same intimate expression? It wasn't exactly the same. But what were the chances? Theresa had received a hydrangea, Johnny's first present to me.

A clear truth struck me then. *None of this was meant to happen here, at Eris's house.* The plant was meant to go to Theresa, while her husband was away. I looked around at each person, seeking a sign that anyone else was thinking what I was thinking. They were all smiling. Perhaps I was the only paranoid person in the room. The concussion had done a number on my brain.

Theresa flung her arms around Kadin's neck, kissing him on the lips. "Thank you, sweetie!"

He remained stiff, unyielding. When she let go of him, a shadow of confusion crossed his face, and then he took the card from Theresa and read it to himself, then gave the card back to her. "You're welcome."

"What's the occasion?" Eris said. "Are you going to spill? Birthday? Anniversary?"

Theresa looked down at her hands in her lap, and her face turned a deep shade of pink. She looked up at Kadin, and he nodded slightly, as if giving her permission to speak. She smiled shyly at everyone and bit her lip.

"It's been a secret the last couple of months, until we could be sure things were going well. And they are, so we can tell you. Kadin and I are expecting our second child in the spring."

"What? Congratulations!" Eris exclaimed. She burst up from the table and ran around to hug Theresa and Kadin. He smiled distantly. Congratulations were dispensed all around, and even I got up to hug Theresa and Kadin, although I had only just met them. I was happy for Theresa, happy for her good news, but her pregnancy also accentuated my own emptiness. My throat felt parched, but I kept smiling—what else could I do?

Johnny smiled in his magnetic way and raised his wineglass. "A toast," he said grandly. "To romance, new neighbors, and happy family surprises."

"A toast," everyone said and raised their glasses in unison.

CHAPTER THIRTEEN

When I arrived at Harriet's house in the afternoon, the neatness had fallen victim to the whims of a little girl who had spilled juice on the carpet, left a sprinkling of crumbs on the countertop, and pulled picture books off the shelves. Her greasy fingerprints had christened every available surface, including the remote control for the television, doorknobs, and the kitchen table. A dusting of flour on the countertops hinted at a recent baking experiment. Puzzle pieces were scattered on the coffee table, a jungle animal tableau beginning to form from chaos.

Harriet had left in a hurry, late for her appointment, with vague instructions to let Mia take a nap if she needed one, to give her animal crackers and juice if she got hungry. She sat on the living room carpet, a jumble of crayons laid out on the coffee table, scribbling in a Disney princess coloring book with her tongue protruding from her mouth. Her hair looked more jaggedly cut today, as if a miniature lawnmower had gone berserk on her head.

I sat on the couch, distracted. When Johnny and I had returned to the cottage the previous night, I'd mentioned the note in the hydrangea, its phrasing similar to the words we had shared for nearly three years. Johnny had denied knowing anything about the flower delivery.

Why would he? He'd apologized for not sending me flowers, and in the morning, he'd brought me coffee with plain soy milk. He knew exactly what I liked. Browned toast, never burned. Smooth, creamy peanut butter, no salt added.

"Look, the queen's eyes are . . . purple!" Mia was coloring outside the lines, creating new shapes beyond the Disney boundaries.

"Good for her," I said.

Mia dropped the purple crayon, picked up indigo, began coloring in the princess's gown. "And blue."

"You know your colors."

"This picture is for my mommy." Mia ripped the page out of the coloring book and held it up for me to see.

I smiled sadly. "Beautiful."

Mia turned the page to the outlines of happy bunnies and fawns. "This one is for my daddy."

"It's nice that everyone gets a picture."

"Nana, too," Mia said solemnly.

"Nana, too." Monique survived in the flourish of Mia's arm as she reached for a green crayon to color the trees. She drew a little heart and a few squiggles above the forest. "And one for you."

"Thank you," I said softly.

She pointed to the squiggles. "It says 'I love you.'"

"I love you, too, sweetie."

She grinned at me, then flipped the page again. "One for my teacher."

"You can't forget your teacher!" With a sting of tears in my eyes, I got up and organized the books on the shelves, straightening up. Harriet's room, right across from Mia's, was still tidy—frilly rose bedspread, pink curtains, even a dressing table with a rose carving on the wood above the mirror.

In the guest room across the hall, a single bed was pushed up against the wall, a sewing table and machine in the opposite corner, fabric and patterns piled on a chair next to a desk and a filing cabinet. I checked back on Mia again. She was still coloring, so I returned to the guest room, drawn by the stack of papers, sympathy cards, and files on the desk. Aware of my nosiness, and touched by guilt, I nevertheless looked through the cards from doctors, teachers, Harriet's old friends, her family on the East Coast. A manila folder caught my eye. It was labeled "Mia." Inside were copies of Mia's medical records, and beneath the medical records, a copy of her birth certificate. Mia had weighed seven pounds, one ounce. She had been born at 2:35 a.m. at Cove Hospital on February 13. Her mother was Monique Beaumont, but no father was listed. Not even a blank line for the father's name.

Nothing at all.

CHAPTER FOURTEEN

On the drive back to Shadow Bluff Lane, I found myself making a detour, turning into Eris's driveway. I tried to process what I had just learned about Mia. I'd assumed Chad was her biological father, but what if my assumption had been wrong? Monique had mentioned a quick wedding four years ago, which meant Mia might have already been born when Monique and Chad had tied the knot. In any case, Mia's parentage was nobody's business.

When Harriet had returned home, she'd asked me to take Mia for the night the following weekend. She had to return to the hospital for more extensive tests. She'd looked drawn and tired, like a walking wisp.

I had agreed. But we didn't own any toys or books, and there was no place for Mia to sleep in the cottage, so I'd called Eris to ask if we could borrow an extra bed, and now, when I approached the newly painted porch, I found Todd Severson working on the railing, hammer in hand. His dark hair, the angles of his face, seemed to absorb the sunlight.

"Go on, she's upstairs exercising," he said. He gave me a long, penetrating look.

"Thanks," I said. "Maybe I shouldn't disturb her?"

He sat back on his heels. "You gonna carry the bed yourself?"

My cheeks flushed. "I hadn't thought of that."

"It's heavy. She said I should help you out."

"I appreciate that. I wanted to ask you what you meant—"

"About what?"

"You were about to tell me something before."

"Nope. Don't remember that." He returned to hammering again.

Fine, then. Maybe he had nothing to tell me. I opened the heavy front door and went inside. Eris's house felt cool, drafty. The overwhelming smell of orange polish wafted through the air, a reminder of Sunday mornings on Sitka Lane, when I'd made freshly squeezed orange juice. The memory followed me up the wide staircase to the second floor.

A thumping, repetitive drumbeat came from a room at the end of the hall. Several framed photos lined the walls. Landscapes—forest and ocean vistas—and a photograph of Eris as a teenager, standing between a man and woman with kind faces, probably her parents. Soft, classical music emanated from a room to my left. I knocked, but nobody answered. The door was locked. I waited a moment, listening. Opposite kinds of music were coming from the other end of the hall.

The drumbeat stopped, and Eris emerged. "Sarah! I didn't hear you come in."

"Sorry—I—Todd said to—"

"Of course. The bed." Eris smiled as she strode toward me, springing on the balls of her feet. She nodded at the room with the locked door. "That's my quiet room. I was in my Zumba room." Her skintight Lycra exercise pants shone, a sweatband around her forehead. "Come on. Follow me." Eris led me across the hall, into an extra bedroom that had become a storage room. She dragged out a cot from behind a large framed photograph of the Seattle Space Needle. "Camp cot, see, folds out."

"Perfect," I said. "I appreciate this."

"I was saving this for my boyfriend. I think he would love camping." She winked at me as we maneuvered the cot past obstacles toward the door.

"Oh? A boyfriend?"

Eris gave me a conspiratorial look. "Don't tell anyone. I'm still in the middle of my divorce. I know, I move fast."

I smiled. "Good for you. Congratulations."

"He's still caught up in difficult entanglements. But the pieces will fall into place, and we'll be together." She reached the door, shouldered it open.

"I hope everything goes smoothly."

"So do I."

We carried the cot downstairs and out onto the deck. The bed felt surprisingly heavy. Todd hoisted the cot over his shoulder and strode to his blue truck.

"I could meet you over there later, if you have time for a walk in the woods?" Eris said. "I could show you the trail to the river."

"Great. I'll see you there."

I waved good-bye to Eris and drove back to the cottage, with Todd following in his truck. He took the cot inside and set it up for me in the extra bedroom. He picked up a photograph from the table. It was a picture of Monique, Chad, Johnny, and me skating on the only ice rink in town, two winters earlier. I'd forgotten about the photo. Johnny had kept it in his wallet. Todd stared at the picture and frowned, sadness in his eyes. "The fire burned so damned hot." I could almost see the flames reflected in his eyes. Then his face crumpled, and a tear slipped down his cheek.

I had no idea what to say. A stranger had never fallen apart in front of me. "I'm sorry" was all I could manage. "You did the best you could."

"Yeah." He wiped his eyes and strode to the door, his face red with embarrassment. "Sorry. That was crazy."

"Don't worry. It's okay. We're all human."

He opened the door, then looked back at me. "You got a house yet?" He looked toward the Minkowskis' A-frame, then back at me.

"No. Why?"

"When you get a house, move as far from this town as you can."

"Why would we want to do that?" Numbness spread inward from my fingertips. "Do you know something about the fire? Why would we want to leave town?"

He seemed to snap out of his trance. He looked at me, his eyes bloodshot, haunted. "If I was you, and I knew some crazy asshole was trying to burn me down, I'd want to get the heck out of Dodge." He strode to his truck, and I ran after him.

"Is that what you wanted to tell me before?"

He got in, started the engine with the door still open. "Don't tell anyone I said that, okay?"

"But why?"

He sighed, closing the door. He rolled the window down. "All's I know is, if it was me, I would be gone." And then he was.

CHAPTER FIFTEEN

"But you and Johnny can't leave town!" Eris had come over to take me for a hike. She wore a heavy knit sweater, hiking slacks, and boots. Even in outdoor gear, she looked perfectly dressed, like a catalogue model for L.L.Bean.

"Why do you think Todd would say that?" I felt ordinary in a heavy red sweater, jeans, and running shoes.

"He knows arsonists try again. Happened once on his watch. Jealous boyfriend tried to burn down his girlfriend's house, succeeded the second time, before they caught him. Todd was called out on that incident."

"That might explain things. But who knows what the motive was for the fire on Sitka Lane?"

"He's being protective. He has a soft side to him. The day after the fire, he didn't come over to work on the deck. He said he wasn't feeling well."

"The poor man. He shouldn't feel responsible."

"He shouldn't, but . . . it wears on him."

"I left a message for the fire marshal. I thought he should know about my conversation with Todd."

Eris nodded thoughtfully as she led me across the street, into the cool, crisp day. The edges of the clouds glowed, but there was still no sign of rain. We passed the Minkowskis' house, the garden strewn with toys and a small bicycle. The cars were gone. Then Eris veered right, into the thickest part of the woods.

"The trail widens a ways down," she said, "but for now, we have to walk single file."

I followed her, watching her jerky, athletic strides, her determination, as if she were late for an appointment.

As the road disappeared behind us, we seemed suddenly to enter deep wilderness, miles from civilization, the birds twittering, clicks and chirps beneath the huckleberry bushes. The smells of the forest pulled me back to childhood, when I'd spent much of my time in the woods, looking for wildlife, little field mice and caterpillars, writing notes in my journal. In my new journal, a postfire diary, I'd started jotting notes, emotions, impressions.

The rush of the river grew closer, louder beyond the thick forest of firs and cedars.

"This whole area is greenbelt," Eris called over her shoulder. "The Shadow Cove reserve right down to the river."

"Beautiful!" I shouted back. The trail was wide enough now for me to catch up and fall into step beside her. The air smelled of leaves and moss, sweet and clean.

"What happened with Todd's wife?" I asked.

"Up and left him. He was so in love with her when they first met, he said, but then she changed. Do we change after we're married?"

"Johnny and I stayed pretty much the same, I think." But did we?

"How did the two of you meet?" Eris stopped at the high bank of the river. The dark water flowed below in complex currents.

"Annual polar bear plunge. He's got a T-shirt commemorating the occasion."

Eris grinned, her face lighting up. "I love the plunge. I've done it twice, got a T-shirt, too."

"You're brave. I never had the guts to make the leap. The water's too cold. But I watched other brave souls dive in." I shivered at the memory. "I gave Johnny a beach towel. He'd forgotten his. Can you believe it? That was how we started talking."

"Over ice water. Romantic. I met my ex-husband at the county fair on the hippo ride. We squeezed into the same booth. The other booths were all taken. I held on to him as the darned thing swung around and around."

"That's quite a story; trumps mine."

"I specialize in trumping." We followed the meandering trail along the high bank, the occasional path branching off down toward the river. "In the end, stories didn't help us," she continued after a bit. "We're still mired in our nasty divorce."

"I'm sorry."

"It's better this way. We weren't meant to be together."

Were Johnny and I meant to be together? I'd accepted his marriage proposal after much thought, after we'd fallen deeply, irrevocably, fiercely in love. But now I wondered, had I waited long enough? It would not do to entertain any questions. Not when we'd lost everything and needed to be strong together.

Eris led me to a spectacular waterfall. A spray of white water cast a mist through the air, a faint rainbow hovering in the sky. The river dropped off precipitously here, churning at the bottom of the rocky falls, then grew calmer a distance downstream.

She pointed out a narrow trail offshoot up on the right. "That way goes to the Minkowskis' place. You have to remember all the turns. I accidentally went that way once and eventually got dumped into their garden. I've practiced retracing the route. Easy to get lost on the way." The entrance to the trail was marked by a lush wild rhododendron.

"Johnny would love this trail," I said.

"Oh, he already knows it. This is where I saw him that day he was running."

"You're kidding."

"I was a ways behind him. Couldn't catch up. But when I got to the end of the route, there he was, in the Minkowskis' garden, chatting with Theresa."

"Maybe he had gotten lost. You know, guys hate to ask for directions until it's too late."

We both laughed, but my laughter felt forced. The air grew colder, the breeze turning into a strong wind. Yes, Johnny had done exactly what Eris had done. He'd gotten lost, wandered off onto the wrong trail, the one that circuitously led to the Minkowskis' yard, entirely by accident.

CHAPTER SIXTEEN

The next morning, when Johnny left for his jog, I watched him race across the street to the trail. What made me leave my coffee mug on the counter, throw on my running shoes, and follow him? A cool autumn wind whipped through the trees, muffling my footfalls. The Minkowski house was dark, no cars in the driveway.

As I sprinted down the trail, I scanned the woods for Johnny, but I couldn't see him. What if he'd turned off onto another trail? I picked up my pace, my lungs protesting. How could I have fallen so far out of shape?

Towhees twittered in the underbrush. Where the trail descended toward the river, I spotted Johnny far ahead. As he slowed to look at his cell phone, I slipped behind a tree. *Just catch up with him, talk to him,* I thought, but some primal instinct held me back.

He tapped the phone with his thumbs, texting someone, then he veered sharply to the right, disappearing into the forest. I raced to catch up. I followed a distance behind as Johnny took several turnoffs. I tried to remember the way. Eventually, he climbed a hill and disappeared on the other side. I stopped at the top, the damp breeze in my hair portending a storm. I hid behind a fir tree, half in shadow, and watched him descend into the Minkowskis' backyard. It was as though I were watching a stranger. He looked so unfamiliar, the way he hunched his shoulders, glancing furtively right and left, then scuttled to the Minkowskis' back door.

I held my breath, the scene in front of me surreal. Theresa answered the door in a shiny pink robe and slippers, her luxurious hair a tousled mess. Instinctively, I reached up to touch my own hair. I could run down the hillside right now, drag everything out into the open. I had half believed, had *wanted* to believe, that Eris had not seen Johnny take this particular route.

Theresa ushered Johnny inside. He took off his knit jogging cap, ducked his head, and went in the back door. He shut the door behind him.

I remained on the hill, the wind cold on my skin. What would I find if I went down to the Minkowskis' house? Johnny and Theresa might be in bed together, their clothes strewn across the floor. Theresa might answer the door naked, or in only a robe. Or not at all. Could Johnny truly be capable of this type of deception? Could he live two lives?

If I had not trampled through the rubble of our house on Sitka Lane, if the walls had not burned down, would I ever have found the photograph of the unidentified woman, the one who had written *my love* on the back of the picture? Would I have ended up here, at the cottage, watching Johnny go in the back door of some strange, married woman's house?

As I stood on that shadowy, wooded hillside, I decided not to make a scene. I would wait until he got home and simply ask him the question, give him the benefit of the doubt.

I didn't want to walk through the Minkowskis' yard—Theresa and Johnny might see me through the window, and he would know I'd been following him. So I turned around and headed back down the trail, my face wet with tears and the first raindrops of autumn.

CHAPTER SEVENTEEN

I retraced my path through the woods. The sky darkened, the rain forming a translucent curtain across the trail. Minuscule droplets of water hit the leaves in staccato beats, like the tiny footfalls of invisible creatures. The river rushed in the distance, fed high in the foothills by Lake Wakhiakum. Now, mingling with the sound of rain, the noise of the waterfall seemed to come from numerous directions, as if its route changed with the wind.

Perhaps I should've taken a different path. I had already broken a promise by clandestinely following my husband. *You can always trust me*, he'd said on our honeymoon. *Never question my love for you.* I had replied, *I promise*, and he had squeezed my hand, his gaze clear and unflinching. *I want this marriage to work, so you have to talk to me. Tell me everything that's on your mind. Right away. Don't hide anything. Don't omit any details.* Johnny would have a good explanation.

The branching paths seemed to multiply in the quickening rain. Which turns had he taken? Eris had known the way as well, but then, she'd lived in her house for a while. We had only just moved into the cottage. If Johnny had wanted to talk to Theresa, why hadn't he simply taken the road again?

Without the compass on my cell phone, I lost all sense of direction. Usually, my brain kept north, south, east, and west roughly in place, but without the sun or landmarks, and without my usual sharpness of thought, I must've passed the first turnoff. The needle point of a headache pierced the back of my skull. The aftereffects of the concussion still addled my judgment. Made me lose my way.

I came upon a vine maple, a splash of bright red in the dreariness of autumn. I had not passed the tree on my way in, or perhaps I had, but I hadn't noticed it, so intent had I been on keeping Johnny in view. Vine maples proliferated in my mother's garden in Portland, an oasis of wilderness outside the city limits.

I love the fall colors in the woods here! Natalie had said to me on the phone, after she had moved to Shadow Cove to work as a hospital nutritionist. I'd still been living in Seattle, had snagged my first book contract, and I'd longed to escape the city, to return to the forest, where my mind could find room to create stories. *You would love it here,* Natalie had said. *So many flowers and trees, right on the ocean.* And so I had moved to Shadow Cove, where my career had blossomed, where I had met Dr. Johnny McDonald. I'd been barely twenty-five; he'd been thirty-four, establishing a private dermatology clinic with two male colleagues. Dr. Johnny McDonald, a dashing bachelor, friend of Natalie's husband, Daniel Kemp, family physician. They had all gone to the annual polar bear plunge, where my offer of a towel to Johnny had set our love in motion. We got married nearly two years later.

Now I could hear the river in motion below. I'd taken an unfamiliar, narrow trail that descended over rocky ground toward the shore. I was going the wrong way, but if I could reach the riverbank, I could turn left and follow the waterline back to the main trail.

The rain had let up by the time I reached the bottom of the trail. I'd wandered off course, downstream from the dangerous waterfall. Here, the river widened into a deceptively serene, glassy pool, although I could sense the current underneath, discernible in faint ripples reaching the surface. The waterfall crashed and roared a distance to my left on the route back to the cottage.

Johnny would surely be ready for work by the time I returned. He would be the one with questions. I imagined him bouncing his car keys in his hand, the way he did when he was impatient, ready to go. *Where have you been? Were you following me?*

At the riverbank, the path flattened, scuffed by many footprints. A thick rope hung from a tree leaning over the water. The embankment descended gently to a narrow, sandy beach. On the opposite bank, an abandoned wooden canoe lay upside down in the grass, its blue paint peeling. And several yards to the right of the boat was a makeshift dock with a broken-down building perched on top. There was something familiar about the layout of the scene—the dock, the building, the cedar and fir trees in the background. The shed was made of weathered, grayed wood, the roof buckling in places, the small, square windows like hollowed-out eyes. An old fisherman's hut, I thought. Chum salmon had once numbered in the thousands, returning from the sea to spawn along the river each winter, drawn by some unknown force of nature, driven to mate, lay their eggs, and die. The salmon would return again in a month or two, but their numbers had diminished.

My sense of reality had diminished, too, wavering on the edge of a dream. I realized, now, why the vista looked familiar. If I were to replace the mist with a brilliant blue summer sky, I could see Johnny sitting on that dock, dangling his feet in the water, the stunning woman in the black bikini sitting beside him, her arm touching his. I could see the fisherman's shed in the background. But no, this could not be the place where the photograph had been taken. There were many rivers in the state, hundreds of lakes, many broken-down shacks. Johnny would have remembered if the photograph had been taken here, so close to the cottage, on the Shadow River.

CHAPTER EIGHTEEN

I had expected to find Johnny ready for work, but when I arrived at the cottage, shivering in my thin outerwear, he was whistling in the shower. How could he act so casual? Maybe he had nothing to hide, and I was the one seeing the world through a tinted lens, my distrustful mind damaged by tragedy and head trauma.

The clock on the kitchen wall indicated that only forty-five minutes had passed since I'd left. Somehow, I thought I'd been gone much longer. Time had slowed in the forest. But inside the cottage, the day sped up. The air thickened, warm and oppressively humid. Johnny ran the shower too hot. Steam emanated from the bathroom, fogging up the living room windows. The smell of lavender soap filled the air.

I'd left the photograph on the table in the second bedroom, the room he now used as an office, but I could not find the picture anywhere. I needed to compare the image to the scene at the river. But no luck.

I went into the bathroom. "I'm back," I said with false cheer. "How was your run?"

"How was your walk? Long one today."

"I got lost," I said. "I ended up on a strange path."

"Bad girl. You didn't take your phone."

"I didn't think I would need it."

"Always take your phone."

"I will next time."

He peered out from behind the shower curtain. His hair was full of soap, water running down his body, flattening the dark hair on his chest. "Is it raining out there?"

"Yes." I looked down at myself, and I realized I was soaked.

"Get in with me. Hurry." He grinned at me in his devilish way. *Come on, a quickie.*

I peeled off my clothes and joined him beneath the hot, soothing water. The cold and rain had sunk into my bones; I leaned back into him, closed my eyes, and felt his hands caressing my body, awakening my nerve endings in the heat. Gradually, I stopped shivering. "I saw you," I said, as he kissed the back of my neck.

"Mmm," he said, kissing my shoulder.

"I mean I followed you," I said.

He kissed my neck again, cupped my breasts in his hands. "Why didn't you yell at me? I would've waited for you."

"I followed you all the way to the Minkowskis' yard and I saw you go in the back door. I saw her let you in."

His hands dropped away from me. "You did?"

"What were you doing there?" I turned to face him. The tub was too small for both of us. Too small and slippery. I could so easily fall and hit my head again.

He blinked, his eyes darkening. "She asked me to stop by," he said after a moment's hesitation. "I took a look at Kadin Junior. She was nearly hysterical about his rash. Allergic reaction. He'll be fine."

"She's lucky you're willing to make house calls." Was he telling me the truth? I realized, looking into his eyes, that I could not read him.

"Sarah, you don't think . . . You couldn't . . ." He tilted my chin up, forcing me to look into his eyes. "You think I went over there to . . . Come on."

"How do I know? I wake up in the night and you're over there, and now you take this backward route through the woods, like you know the way."

"I jog in the woods every day," he said, wrapping his arms around me, pulling me close. "I used to jog out here before I met you. Yeah, I ended up there once before. I remember routes. No big deal. She called the clinic and the call was routed to me. I was already out. So I went over there."

"That's it?"

"That's it, I swear. Why didn't you come down there? You let this fester. You're imagining things."

"It's my job to imagine things. I'm a writer."

"One of the many reasons I love you."

"The picture of you on the dock with that woman. Did you do something with it?"

"What picture? Oh yeah. No, why?"

"I can't find it. You don't remember it—?"

"No, I don't," he said quickly. He was rinsing off now, preparing to get out of the shower.

"I ended up down at the river. Was the picture taken there, at the dock?"

"Show me again . . . I'll see." When he looked at me, his brow was furrowed, his expression guarded.

"The picture's gone," I said.

"I didn't do anything with it," he said, his voice edged with irritation. "What's with all the questions?"

"There was a building in the picture, a fisherman's shed. I saw a similar building today. It looked like the same one."

"It might be. I'm not sure."

"You really don't remember?"

"What does it matter? Look, you're sensitive. I get that. But I'm not lying to you."

"Don't blame this on my childhood," I said.

"But that's what this is about." He got out of the shower, leaving me alone beneath the cooling water.

His words stung, but he was right. When my father had walked out on my mother and me, he had abandoned his past, his entire life. His wife and daughter. He had traded his family in for a younger model. I'd told myself I would not care, I would not mind that he only sent cards and gifts on special occasions, when he remembered. He had moved to London, as far from us as he could get. I could still feel the wound, close to the surface, too easily opened again.

CHAPTER NINETEEN

"Johnny's having an affair. Is that what you want me to say?" Natalie's voice crackled, as if she were even farther away than India, as if she were on the moon.

"You're making me paranoid." Tears pressed at the backs of my eyes.

"You're creating paranoia all by yourself," Natalie said. "Do you seriously believe he would sleep with your pregnant neighbor?"

"He said he didn't."

"Then he didn't."

"You're right. You have to be right." I paced in the cottage, tidying up the few things that already made the place messy—papers and pens, cups and plates, and glossy new copies of the Miracle Mouse latest release, which had arrived that morning in a box. Normally, I would be delighted to see my new book in print, but I felt only a passing thrill.

"Johnny would not fool around on you. He loves you more than life. You remember that chick he went to school with, the one who got drunk and threw herself at him at your wedding?"

"I'd like to forget," I said.

"He only had eyes for you, always has. He's so intensely in love with you, and I am so jealous."

"But the wife is always last to know."

"Your mom was, but it doesn't mean you will be. Not every man on the planet is like your peripatetic, AWOL dad. There's nothing to know about Johnny. You chose him for a reason."

"But our lives feel fragile, Nat. We lost everything. I can't lose him, too."

"You won't."

"Is this one of your predictions?"

"A good one."

I felt as though someone was reaching into my head and twisting my brain around. "I trust him. But what if I shouldn't?"

"You need to focus on healing, getting back on your feet, getting into a house."

When I hung up, I paced. I wasn't going to visit Theresa. I would end up interrogating an innocent, friendly, pregnant neighbor. Natalie was right. Johnny and I needed to look for another place to live. I called Eris to take her up on her offer to show us houses for sale.

***

By Friday afternoon, she had shown us several lovely homes, none of which seemed right. One artsy blue bungalow, hugging the shore of Moon Cove, had too many windows. The scents of outside seeped through the cracks—the salty ocean and a nearby bonfire emitting the nauseating odor of burning wood. At one time, I would've found such a smell comforting, a reminder of campfires and s'mores, but not now. In the bathroom, I had gazed up through the skylight and watched the skittering clouds overhead, while Eris and Johnny chatted in the bedroom. "Dixondale wanted all his windows facing the water," Eris had said. "High glass to let in the most light."

"Art Dixondale designed this house?" Johnny's voice had risen in admiration. They'd discussed one architect after another, and then Eris had shown us a two-story house on Green Spot, the lower level built into the hillside, its rooms dark, the bottom level slightly dank and mildewed. Aside from the view of the ferryboat chugging across Puget Sound, the house had offered nothing to recommend it. We were back where we started. It would take time to find the proper home.

Johnny had started running on the roads, avoiding the woods. It was as though he deliberately followed well-traveled paths in plain view, to reassure me. My headaches started to decrease, but my nightmares took on a life of their own, and it was all I could do to put on a smiling face to babysit Mia on Friday afternoon. Her hair had begun to grow back, but the white scar on her forehead still peeked through her bangs. On the drive from Harriet's place to the cottage, Mia sang along to a Taylor Swift tune playing on the radio.

"Pretty impressive," I said. "Do you know what those words really mean?"

"They're about breaking up with a boy."

"You're full of wisdom," I said as I turned onto Shadow Bluff Lane.

"I'm full of . . . breakfast!"

"Then we can move right along to having fun."

When Johnny got back to the cottage that evening, Mia sat on the living room floor, covered in cookie icing, her hair done up and her nails painted. She quietly played with her Barbie dolls.

Johnny hung his coat in the small front closet and strode into the living room. I sat on the couch, pretending to read, but I watched Mia, who was lost in her Barbie world. Her lips kept moving, her words silent as she engaged the dolls in secret conversation.

"Mia, Uncle Johnny is here," I said.

Mia didn't reply, just kept playing and whispering to herself.

"Hello, Mia." Johnny kneeled next to her, picked up a blond Barbie clad in a pink tutu. "Who is this?"

"That's Barbie I Can Be a Ballerina." She didn't look at him.

"What do you want to be?"

"I'm a princess."

"You certainly are. Nice hairdo."

She looked up at him and smiled, dimples forming in her cherubic cheeks. "I have Barbie Flower 'N Flutter Fairy Doll at home. Not at my grandma's house."

"I see." Johnny glanced up at me, and I shook my head. None of Mia's dolls had survived the fire.

He put the doll down. "We might have to get a replacement."

"No, I have one already. My mommy got it. She's getting me more fairy dolls." She busied herself undressing another Barbie that she'd brought from Harriet's house. "I want Barbie the Princess and the Pop Star."

"You do, do you?" Johnny glanced at the pile of picture books on the coffee table. "Did you bring bedtime stories, too?"

"My daddy reads to me." Mia's lips turned down, and for a moment, she seemed about to burst into tears. Was she remembering the fire? "My daddy is buying me presents. I have Rock Princess Barbie. She has a coloring book. I need more crayons. My favorite color is Granny Smith apple."

"Okay, we'll get Granny Smith apple." He got up and went into the kitchen. I followed. He sifted through the mail, his shoulders tense. "How long is she staying, again?" he asked.

"Overnight," I whispered.

"She still believes she's going home."

"She's only four."

Mia was suddenly silent in the living room, as if she were listening. "Eris mentioned a house for sale up in Kingston," he said. He ripped open envelopes and threw junk mail into the recycling bin.

"I'm taking Mia shopping tomorrow," I said. "Jessie is coming with us."

"Sounds nice," Johnny said absentmindedly.

"You have to work."

"Yes, work." He spoke from another planet.

I returned to the living room, suppressing my irritation, and smiled at Mia. "Want to go on the tire swing before dark?"

Mia jumped to her feet in the carefree manner of children—limbs loose, her head tilted to the side as she held Ballerina Barbie upside down. "Can she come, too?"

"She can come. But you might need both hands on the swing."

"Okay." Mia dropped Barbie on the floor. "She says she wants the Barbie Dreamhouse. It's got a kitchen with a light-up oven and stuff."

"Maybe she should ask your grandma." I took Mia's hand, and it was a major operation to put on her shoes. Johnny escaped into the second bedroom and shut the door. Mia chattered on about the dolls she had at home. She recited all their names.

In the backyard, I helped Mia climb into the tire swing. "It's a donut swing!" she exclaimed, pumping her legs. I'd been pushing her for only a few minutes when Mia pointed toward the road. "Look! A doggy!"

"We don't have any dogs here." But someone's yellow lab pranced around the yard, tongue lolling, whole body wagging.

"Cute doggy!" Mia said, fearless.

"It must belong to a neighbor. Stay here." I ran around to the front. Eris sauntered down the road next to a tall, casually dressed man who held a leash in his hand. "Hey, Sarah!" Eris called out and waved.

Was this the new boyfriend? I met them at the curb, the dog weaving around their legs. Close up, the man had a clean-cut, suave appeal. He called for his dog, *Briana,* in a stern voice, clipped her collar to the leash.

Eris patted Briana's head, then smiled at me, her cheeks flushed. "Sarah, I'd like you to meet Steve Wessler."

I smiled and shook his hand. "Pleased to meet you."

Steve nodded in a perfunctory way, his lips pursed tight, like a horizontal crack in concrete. "We should get back," he said to Eris. "We have things to discuss."

"Yes, things to discuss." Eris winked at me and the couple headed for home, the dog on a short leash.

When I returned to the backyard, I found the tire swinging gently without Mia inside. She couldn't have climbed down so fast on her own.

"Mia, where are you?" A surge of adrenaline kicked me into action. I called for her while I checked behind the woodpile, behind the small shed at the edge of the yard. The door was secured with a padlock. I looked along the edge of the woods. *Okay, don't panic.*

Finally, I heard a small whimpering sound beneath the front porch. Mia hid there, crouched with her arms around her legs. "There you are," I said, relief washing through me.

"I'm scared," she said.

"Nothing's going to happen to you. I promise." But could I really make such assurances? "What would make you feel less scared?"

She looked up at me. "My mom gives me a protection kiss."

Monique's sad eyes materialized in my mind, but I could no longer picture the details of her face. "A double protection kiss for you," I said, and I blew a kiss to Mia. "Will you come out now?"

"Maybe," she said.

"What if I add ice cream to the kiss?"

She nodded and slowly crawled out from under the porch. I held her tight, stroking her soft hair.

Johnny had not come out the whole time. He'd holed up in the office, and later that evening, as I stood in the office doorway, listening to him read *Where the Wild Things Are* to Mia, I no longer felt certain about him as a future father.

At precisely what moment had my feelings begun to shift? I had always imagined him like this, reading to a child. Had he changed, or had I simply become less sure of him?

"Read it again," Mia said when Johnny had finished.

"We've already read it twice," he said wearily.

"Again." What was it about children and repetition? I remembered checking out the same Curious George books from the library again and again when I was a child, seeking the comfort of familiar yellow covers. If only I could find that comfort again.

"Okay, but this is the last time, and then night-night," Johnny said. He read through the story, his deep voice a soothing lullaby. Mia's eyes focused on the full-page, imaginative illustrations, her head resting on his shoulder. Her eyes gradually closed.

As he finished reading, Mia didn't move. She snored softly. Johnny slowly extracted himself from her grasp and got out of bed. I had never seen such a large person move so quietly. Mia did not wake up. Johnny put the book on the table, tiptoed to the door, and turned off the light.

Back in our room, with both doors slightly ajar, Johnny hugged me and stroked my hair. "So, what do you think? Do I make the perfect dad?"

"You were great," I whispered back.

"But not perfect," he said.

"Nobody's perfect."

CHAPTER TWENTY

After Johnny left for work on Saturday, and while Mia played with an elaborate layout of Barbie dolls, Jessie arrived at the cottage in her parents' Honda. She got out of the driver's side in clothing well suited to the weather—black raincoat, gray hoodie, striped beanie, black rain boots. Her face looked puffy from crying, her eyes heavily made up with liner. She smelled of patchouli cologne and lip gloss.

"How are you?" I said, hugging her inside the cottage. "Is everything okay?"

Jessie burst into tears. I handed her a tissue. "Jessie, what is it?"

"I wish I didn't care. I wish I could just, like, hate on him."

"You and Adrian . . . ?"

Jessie wiped her eyes. "He's such a loser."

Maybe she would finally break up with him. "Guys can be that way. I'm so sorry."

Mia hurtled into her arms. "Jessie!"

"Mia! We're going shopping!"

"Yay, for Cinderella shoes?"

"Yes, but you need to put on your regular shoes first. You can't go in socks." Jessie put Mia down.

"They're in the bedroom," Mia said.

Jessie nodded. "Go and get them, then."

"And your jacket," I said.

Mia ran into the bedroom.

Jessie looked around, taking in her surroundings. "This place is totally sick."

"It is fairly small—"

"No, I mean it's sick. I could live here forever. Nobody would know where I was."

"Oh, I get it. Sick as in *good*."

Jessie gave me a funny look, her nose crinkling. "Yeah, what else would I mean?"

Fifteen minutes later, the three of us were heading down into town in my Camry, which I had picked up from the mechanic. Mia chattered the whole way. I parked on Waterfront Road, and we sauntered along the sidewalks, looking into shop windows, Jessie holding Mia's hand, the two lost in earnest conversation. Mia bounced along, gorging on a vanilla ice cream cone, the sticky stuff all over her face, although it was too cold for ice cream. Neatness came with age, I thought, along with the decision to color one's life within the lines.

How long had it been since I had enjoyed a day out on the town, eating pistachio ice cream? Jessie had chosen licorice flavor, a specialty of the downtown creamery. The food coloring turned her mouth green. Every time she stuck out her tongue, Mia yelled, "Ewww, yuck!" and squealed in delight as Jessie chased her down the sidewalk.

"Turns your poop green, too," Jessie said.

"Too much information," I said, rushing after them.

At the Maple Grove Secondhand Boutique, Mia pressed her hands and nose to the window. "Shoes!" she exclaimed, pointing.

"We don't lick the glass," Jessie said. She grabbed Mia's hand and pulled her into the store. I followed.

Mia went straight for the racks of shoes, fascinated by the glitter. She slipped her feet into a pair of black Ferragamos, several sizes too large, and strutted back and forth in front of the full-length mirror. She turned to the side to examine her profile. The store clerk, an elegant woman with delicate features, smiled at me. "Aren't you the writer?"

Heat crept into my cheeks. "One of the many," I said, smiling back.

"But you're the one with a signing coming up at the bookstore. I saw the poster in the window. Books about a mouse detective with a lisp?"

A couple of customers looked up at me. I looked down at my shoes, then smiled at the clerk again. "Yeah, that's me."

"My daughter wants to be a writer—"

"Sparkles!" Mia exclaimed, coming to my rescue. She pulled on a pair of glittering silver slippers in her size.

"You're a gorgeous princess," I said.

She was already running outside.

"Mia!" I ran after her, Jessie close on my heels.

Mia's feet became two flashes of silver as she raced toward the car. "Mia, come back here!" Jessie shouted.

Mia yanked open the car door, got into the backseat.

"Mia, no!" I yelled. The car did not have automatic locks. Jessie must've left the back door unlocked. Mia locked herself inside. Jessie and I rushed to the car, and Jessie banged on the window. "Open up right now."

Mia lifted her right foot and wiggled it. "I'm Cinderella!"

I searched my purse for the keys. Where the hell were they?

"Open the door, baby," Jessie said. "We can't steal shoes. It's dangerous to get in the car by yourself."

Mia shook her head. "I'm Cinderella," she repeated.

I cupped my hands to the window and peered into the car. The keys glinted on the front seat, mocking me. "I'll have to call a locksmith."

Jessie followed my gaze. "Oh no! Wait. I have an idea." She unzipped her shoulder bag, brought out a golden tube of lipstick. "Mia, look here." She held up the lipstick to the window. The initials *M. K.* were engraved on the side. "Remember when we tried on makeup?"

Mia looked up now, her eyes focused on the lipstick.

Monique's voice echoed in my mind. *I kept a gold pen by the phone . . .*

CHAPTER TWENTY-ONE

Jessie pulled out a matching compact, also engraved with the initials *M. K.* She opened the compact, the mirror reflecting a flash of sunlight. "This is magical princess makeup, and it's all for me." She made a show of applying the bright cherry lipstick, admiring herself in the mirror.

Mia flung open the door and emerged without a thought for how she had given us fibrillations. "I want to try," she said, reaching for the lipstick. Then her face contorted into a grimace, and her lips began to tremble. Her eyes misted over with tears. "Mommy," she said in a plaintive voice. "I want Mommy. Where's my mommy? Mommy!"

Instantly, my irritation dissolved. I picked up Mia and held her tightly. "It's okay, honey. We're here."

It took me a while to calm her, and later, after we'd returned Mia to Harriet, I confronted Jessie as I drove her back to the cottage. "You stole from the Kimballs."

In the passenger seat, she breathed vapor on the window, traced a circle with her forefinger on the glass.

"How did you get Monique's makeup?" I asked again.

Jessie shrugged. "She loaned me stuff." She took the lipstick and compact out of her pocket, laid them on the seat. "I was going to give them back."

"Jessie, you realize—"

Her face crumpled. "Please don't tell. I thought she wouldn't mind. I was going out to the Under 21 Club. I was going to put them back right after. I always do. She would never have known I took them. But then she and Chad came back early."

"You can't keep her stuff."

"Why not? She's dead now."

"Jessie . . ."

"Well, she is. They both are." Jessie looked out the window. After a minute, she said, "Do you think she was pretty?"

"Who, Monique?"

"She was a model once. In France."

"She was elegant." Monique's voice floated back to me, the shimmer of her dress, the way she could walk in heels as if gliding on a cloud.

"Do you think her accent was sexy? Like *Le fromage est sur la table*?"

"You've been learning French?"

"I said, 'The cheese is on the table.'"

"That's good. Did you take any other things from Monique? What else do you have?"

Jessie looked down at her fingers adorned with silver rings. Then she looked up at me, her gaze wide-eyed and anxious. "Are you going to tell my parents?"

"That's up to you. You do need to talk to them."

"They'll kill me."

"They might be angry, but they'll get over it."

"I have some other things . . ."

"You can't keep them."

"I know." Jessie twisted her hands together in her lap. "There's one thing . . . It's personal. She wouldn't have wanted anyone to see it."

"What thing?"

"A journal. I couldn't help it. But it didn't tell me anything."

"What do you mean? What was it supposed to tell you?"

"She did say something, but not about . . . what I needed to know."

A chill traveled up my back. "What did you need to know?" I turned onto Shadow Bluff Lane, the trees casting long autumn shadows across the road.

Jessie blinked away tears. "This one time, I was babysitting Mia. I tried on Monique's makeup, just for fun. After Mia went to bed. I put on one of Monique's black bras. I was only messing around. And . . . he came home."

"Who came home?"

"Chad." Jessie stared through the windshield at the dense forest. "I didn't hear him come in. He said he forgot something. He looked like he'd been crying. Like maybe he wanted to get away from Monique. Like they were fighting."

I turned up into the cottage driveway and parked. "How did he react to you? Was he angry?"

"At first, he was kind of shocked. He was like, what are you doing in our room? But then he looked at me in a whole different way."

I went cold. "What way?"

Tears slipped down Jessie's cheeks. She didn't bother to wipe them away. "He said I looked beautiful."

"And . . . ?" Could Chad have exploited this young woman, right under everyone's noses? He'd seemed so friendly, so . . . normal. But then, Ted Bundy had seemed normal to his neighbors, as well.

Jessie's eyes misted over, full of grief and longing. "He said I smelled like his wife. I was wearing her Dior perfume. The bottle was so pretty."

I took a deep breath. "Did he—? Did you—? Did the two of you—?"

"First, he did this." Jessie held her hand near my cheek. "I didn't move. I closed my eyes. I wanted him to touch me."

I tried to keep my voice steady. "What happened next?"

"He kissed me."

"He did?"

Jessie leaned back against the headrest. "He was the best kisser. He didn't tongue me, not the way Adrian does. Adrian slobbers. But Chad, he was gentle."

"He kissed you, and that's it? If something more happened, you can tell me. I'll keep it confidential. Just between you and me."

Jessie looked at me with an expression full of sadness and longing. "He told me to go home."

"That's it?"

"I called him a few times after that. Then he changed his cell phone number. And Monique started looking at me funny, too. It didn't matter what I did, how I dressed, what I said. I wanted him to look at me the way he looked at her. He told me I was beautiful, but I guess I wasn't beautiful enough. I wasn't as beautiful as her."

I had lived right across the street from Jessie, right next door to Chad. I'd seen them both coming and going. But I hadn't really *seen*. "You know it wasn't okay for him to do that. You're underage and Chad . . . He was married." *He took advantage of your naïveté, your immaturity.*

"But I wanted it. It was my decision, too."

You only think it was. "You had a crush on Chad."

Jessie leaned forward, her arms crossed over her abdomen. "It was more than a crush. My heart still hurts, and my stomach, too, like I ate something rotten, like the time I got the flu."

"I'm sorry, sweetie." I bit my tongue to keep from spouting useless advice. "What about Adrian?"

"I didn't tell him, but he knew something was up."

"You stayed with him through all this." Back in my high school days, I had occasionally, shamelessly juggled more than one boyfriend at a time. Not that Chad had been a boyfriend to Jessie, as far as I knew.

"Yeah, but . . ."

"I know it's hard. You're a good person at heart. You deserve a future and happiness." I yanked a tissue from the box on the dashboard and handed it to Jessie.

"So do you," Jessie said, blowing her nose.

"Thank you." *I've forgotten the meaning of happiness.* "Did you start, um, borrowing Monique's things after that encounter with Chad?"

Jessie nodded. "All the guys looked at her. Even Adrian. He said she was hot."

"You wanted to be like her. And then maybe Chad would want you."

Jessie ignored the crumpled tissue in her lap and wiped her nose with the back of her hand. The tears kept coming. "How come she mesmerized everyone? Even Adrian? What did she have that I don't have? I feel bad that I'm even thinking this stuff."

"You don't need to be like her or anyone else. You're fine the way you are."

"Except for stealing, right?"

"You need to talk to your parents and come clean."

"Yeah."

I glanced at my cell phone. It was four o'clock. "Will you be okay driving home in your car? I can take you. We can get the Honda back to you later."

Jessie sat up straight and took a deep breath, shoring up her nerve. "My parents will be home around six. So we have time."

"Time for what?"

"You need to come over. I have to show you something."

CHAPTER TWENTY-TWO

Jessie ushered me into the foreign world of her room, dimly lit by the tepid autumn sun. Her bed was an unmapped sea of wrinkled sheets. An iPod lay on the nightstand next to a black lace bra.

Where was the young Jessie I had known, still in thick glasses and excited about her science projects? The girl who explained the way images flipped upside down on the human retina, before the brain turned the pictures right side up again? Such mysterious mechanics of physiology had always fascinated her—she had talked of becoming an ophthalmologist.

But as her body had begun to mature, she had switched to contact lenses, and I suspected that sometimes, she made do with blurred vision for the sake of vanity. Ironically, her eyes seemed more hidden now behind mascara than they had behind her glasses.

Now she scooped up the bra and tucked it under her pillow in one swift movement. But she could not easily hide evidence of her night forays. A skimpy silver tank top glittered on an armchair. A mound of clothes rose up on the dressing table, next to a jumble of perfume bottles, tubes of lipstick, palettes of eye shadow. A mass of gold necklaces and beads spilled over the edge of a jewelry box.

But across from the bed, along the opposite wall, her childhood picture books squeezed into a tall set of shelves. I recognized Dr. Seuss titles, *The Chronicles of Narnia*, the *Lord of the Rings* trilogy.

"Sorry about the mess," she said, rushing to the chair and grabbing the tank top. She shoved it into a drawer.

I looked around for a place to sit. She hurriedly smoothed the bed, making room on the cover. I sat on the mattress. "Do your parents know?" I asked her. Jessie crouched in front of her desk, which sat next to her bookshelves. Her back was turned to me. "Do they know what?"

"That you're sexually active. I can tell." In fact, I was only guessing.

She searched through her key chain, hesitated a moment. "You make it sound so technical."

"It is technical, in a way."

"It's not about sex."

"Maybe not for you."

"They don't know. Their heads would explode. They would lock me up."

"They wouldn't do that."

"You don't know my parents," Jessie said bitterly. "Once I came home and my mom was in my room. In my space. She said she was doing laundry but that was a gigantic lie. She was snooping."

"Parents do that because they care. I know how that sounds."

"Stupid. It sounds stupid."

"You're using birth control, aren't you?"

"The operative word being *control*. That's what my mom is, a control freak."

"Whatever you do, Jess, do for you. Look at your own dreams. At your conscience."

"My conscience is not compatible with life these days." She used a small brass key to unlock the bottom drawer of her desk.

"Don't say that. You have a good head on your shoulders."

"But I have to learn how to use it, huh?"

"You're too hard on yourself. And on your parents, too. They're doing their best."

"When I turn eighteen, I swear. Only a couple more days."

"You swear what?" I could not disguise the alarm in my voice. Jessie seemed younger than her age.

"Just, I swear, that's all. Darn, damn, shit."

"Jess—"

"My mom almost faints if I say *shit*. But people say a lot worse these days. Like—"

"You were going to say something else about your birthday."

"I don't even want a birthday cake or presents or anything."

She glanced out the window, at the oblique view of what had once been the Kimballs' house. Jessie's room was on the first floor, facing the Calassis house. This room had been the guest room in our house across the street.

"Look, don't do anything rash," I said.

"Why not? Life is short. You never know when you're gonna die, right? You could get burned to death in your sleep."

"Your house is not going to burn down."

"How do you know? You don't know that. You don't know when someone you love with all your heart is going to go up in smoke." Her voice wobbled dangerously close to a cliff.

I realized, then, that even in the midst of her tearful confession of love for Chad, Jessie might've been lying, telling me what I wanted to hear. Had Chad stopped at kissing her? Or had he gone further? Jessie might never tell me the truth. People kept layers of secrets, I realized—the ones held close to the surface, wanting to be revealed, and deeper ones, hidden too far down to be retrieved or sometimes even acknowledged.

Jessie opened her desk drawer and brought out her loot—a glass paperweight with a leaf suspended inside, like an insect in amber; a gold Cross pen; a sample bottle of Dior perfume. A twilight-blue cloth journal with images of migrating geese woven diagonally across the cover.

She sat beside me on the bed, the journal in her lap. "I was going to put it back," she said, "but the Kimballs came home early—"

"Where did you find this?"

Jessie pushed her hair out of her eyes. "She didn't hide it very well. It was in her dresser under the bras."

"But she did hide it. You shouldn't have been rummaging in her drawers."

"I know, but I found it. The cover looked so beautiful and I thought, maybe she wrote something like—I don't know. Like maybe something about Chad wanting a divorce."

"You thought he might get a divorce to be with you." I kept my voice even—I had been naïve once, too. Perhaps I was still naïve in entirely different ways.

"Stupid, right?" Jessie gazed out toward the charred rubble, her eyes red and watery.

"Oh, sweetie, you're not stupid. You're just a teenager with a broken heart." I had been there once, where she was now, when my heart shattered for the first time.

Jessie's lips trembled. "Yeah," she whispered.

"But you can't go rummaging through other people's stuff. You need to give this to the authorities." What authorities did I mean, exactly? What would Ryan Greene do with a private diary? "Or maybe give it to her next of kin."

"Who, Mia?" Jessie wiped her nose with the back of her sleeve. "Not Harriet. Harriet didn't even like Monique."

"You should give it to the police."

"What if I go to juvie? I knew this kid once—"

"Whatever happens, the truth is always the best policy."

"What if I throw it back on the property? The cops could find it there."

"You would know the truth. That you took it. They would know, too. They've already combed the property. The journal is not ours to keep . . . or even to read."

"The cops will read it, too. And I already read it. She's dead, what does it matter?"

"Jess. It matters."

"Whatever." She opened the journal and pointed at the first page. "She talks about a man she was with. Not Chad."

"How do you know that? People write fantasies. Not always reality." The curtains began to slap against the open window, the wind picking up outside.

"Seems pretty real to me. She was sleeping with some guy named Jules."

I inhaled sharply. The pages became porous, sucking up all the oxygen in the room, until I could hardly breathe. "That can't be right." *Is Jules at home?*

"Yeah. She had a boyfriend. A French guy. Jules is a French name, right? Or something?"

"Or something," I said faintly.

"Look. Right here." Jessie transferred the journal to my lap.

On the parchment-like paper, Monique had written Johnny's nickname, Jules, from *Jules and Jim*, the movie we had all watched together. At the end of the movie, Catherine, the *femme fatale*, the woman both men loved, drove her car off a bridge with Jim inside, leaving Jules to deal with the ashes of his friends.

You would be Jules, the quiet one, Monique had told Johnny. *Chad would be Jim, the noisy one.*

And who would be Catherine? I had asked.

Moi, bien sûr.

Monique's flamboyant handwriting slanted across the page, reminiscent of calligraphy from a time when penmanship had been a valued art.

Dear Jules,

We're finally leaving. Our decision fills me with hope but also with grief. To move is to say a final good-bye to you. Mia imagines herself a princess moving into a mythic castle. Jim and I, we will make her dreams come true. If only I could believe in fairy tales as she does. Sometimes, when I see you, memories come back to me. Details. Moments. We agreed that we shared physical pleasure and nothing more. I know what I said, but for me, hearts and bodies could never be separate.

But I have grown to love Jim for his gentleness, compassion, and so much more. My heart and body are with him, at long last.

He never suspected the truth of what happened between you and me, but Harriet has always known. I see the way she looks at me. She thinks I'm a bad mother. She does not understand the depth of my love for Mia and now for Jim, as well. But as long as we stay here, close to you, the past will always be with us.

Jules, I wish . . .

Bonsoir, mon amour.

Monique

CHAPTER TWENTY-THREE

I kneeled to turn over the heavy stone turtle in my mother's front yard. A cold, steady rain seeped beneath the collar of my raincoat, plastered my hair against my head. My teeth chattered, and my fingers were numb. If only my brain would go numb, too. I didn't want to imagine Johnny and Monique together. I didn't want to grieve any more losses.

Where was the damned key? I searched in the wet dirt, my tears mingling with the rain. What if someone had stolen it or my mother had forgotten to leave one out? I would have to stay in a hotel. Or drive all the way back to the cottage after dark.

What if the key had been eaten by a burrowing rodent? Nature seemed to have taken over the property. I'd last been here just before my mother had left for Kenya, but in only a few months, the grass had become overgrown, even with the gardener maintaining the property. Weeds choked out the shrubs. Pine needles and leaves littered the path to the porch.

Finally, I found the key buried in the soil, wrapped inside a Ziploc bag. My mother had always been good at hiding things. Her pain, her grief, her inability to get over my father. She had never remarried. But she traveled.

I was waterlogged now—even my bones felt damp. But the house was warm inside and smelled surprisingly fresh and clean, a hint of lavender in the air. My mother liked to tuck dried herb sachets in drawers. The furniture was functional but comfortable, the décor a museum of mementos from the countries she had visited.

I'd left a message on Johnny's cell phone, and then had nearly thrown my phone across the room. Why was I perpetually leaving messages for him, never reaching him in person?

I'd also left him a note. *I know about Monique. I'm at my mom's house in Portland in case of emergency. But please don't come here. I need time.* So many questions brewed in my mind. Everything I had believed about my life had been merely a magic trick, a curtain of sparkling fairy dust thrown up before my eyes to hide the truth.

My childhood bedroom, with its slanted roof and dormer window overlooking the ravine, felt familiar yet strange. My dresser and desk were still here. My mother had replaced the single mattress with a guest bed. The childhood things I had loved most—my plush stuffed animals, my favorite pens, old coloring books, dolls, Lite-Brite—had been packed away into storage.

A small collection of books remained on the shelves—Nancy Drew mysteries, Beatrix Potter tales, a few college textbooks. I'd eased my way into the writing profession, first penning articles for campus newspapers, then company profiles for coffee table books, then short stories, then novels. Now I had a career, but no life, no husband, and no home.

I lay on the bed and stared up at the textured ceiling. In high school, I had pasted a mural of redwood trees up there, but when I'd left for college, my mother had peeled off the mural and repainted the ceiling. I closed my eyes and tried to recapture an image of the comforting forest, but nothing came to mind. I could not go back.

My cell phone buzzed again. Johnny had left six messages already. I ached to talk to him, to ask him how long he'd been with Monique. When? Was he in love with her? Why had he split up with her?

Was Mia his daughter? So many other moments now took on new meaning: Johnny veering off to Theresa's house, letting calls go to voice mail, the hang-ups, the hushed conversations, not answering his cell phone the night of the fire. But I could not replay every possible instance of infidelity, or I would drive myself crazy.

For now, for a few hours, I needed to nurse my wounds. I took a long, hot bath, changed into a pair of flannel pajamas, made a cup of chamomile tea. And I cried. I'd been crying on and off on the drive down from the peninsula, in the bath, while I'd wandered around the house, touching familiar objects, framed family photographs lined up on the mantel. My house might've burned down, but at least my mother had kept some of my childhood belongings. I still had evidence of my past, even if my entire reality had been turned inside out.

She had also left evidence of her rush for the airport. She hadn't put the cap on the toothpaste. A mug sat on the kitchen counter with a fossilized ring of coffee inside. An unread, folded newspaper lay on the dining table, dated the day she had left.

In my mother's study, I found a pile of photo albums. She still preferred to print hard copies. She'd never been much into technology. But she had removed and discarded every photograph of my father. Except for one. I found the picture of him holding me when I was a chubby baby. He wore swimming trunks on the beach, a pipe protruding from his mouth, his hairline already receding. He smiled at me as if he loved me. But he'd been sleeping with another woman for nearly two years before he had left my mother and me. He hadn't loved us enough to give up his affair.

I closed the album with trembling fingers and pulled out another one labeled WEDDING: SARAH AND JOHNNY. My father had not come to the wedding. But the photographer had captured happiness all the same—my strut down the aisle beneath the tent, since a sprinkling rain had arrived for our June wedding, and we'd hastily set up the shelter at the last minute. Throwing the bouquet. Nearly tripping over my bridal train. The makeup that had made my skin itch. Each of my friends—and Johnny's—had been captured alone or in small groups, holding glasses of champagne, eating cake, chatting.

Later in the evening, we'd danced. In nearly every picture of Johnny and me together, he held my hand tightly, gazing into my eyes. Had his love been real? Our marriage had always felt authentic to me. Could I trust my intuition? Not with all the gaps, the questions, the proof of his affair.

I lingered over a photograph of the two of us at dinner, at the wedding reception. Why hadn't I noticed Monique in the background, at the next table, in a revealing green sleeveless dress? She seemed to be posing for the camera. She rested her chin in her hand, her head turned slightly to the side. Her hair was done up elaborately, her gold earrings glinting. She laughed at something someone said off-camera, but she stared at the back of Johnny's head. Had the two of them been sleeping together even then?

It didn't help to keep imagining the worst. Sleep would help. Numb and exhausted, I retreated to bed and curled up in a fetal position, my arms around my knees. When I had half drifted off, I heard a loud knocking on the front door. I sat up straight, my heartbeat erratic. My head felt fuzzy. The doorbell rang. I knew who it was. I considered not answering, but I couldn't avoid him forever.

CHAPTER TWENTY-FOUR

I couldn't help the irrational rush of anticipation as I hurried down the stairs and peered through the keyhole, just to be sure.

Johnny's distorted eye stared back at me, and when I opened the door, he stood on the porch like a large, bedraggled drifter, an impossibly alluring one. His breath condensed into steam in the cold air. I wanted to hug him and pummel him all at once. Love him and kill him.

"What are you doing here?" I said. "It's the middle of the night."

"I drove as fast as I could. There's construction on I-5."

"I told you not to come."

"You wanted me to come, or you wouldn't have told me where you were." He reached out to touch my cheek, gently, as if I were a breakable object. And I let him. "Can I come in?"

I couldn't slam the door in his face. I stepped back and crossed my arms over my chest. He brushed past me, and I closed and locked the door. He took off his coat and hung it in the closet. He knew where everything was in this house. He'd been here for Christmas, birthdays, Thanksgiving, rites of passage that repeated themselves every year.

He went into the living room and sat on the couch, dark circles beneath his eyes. "Why did you run away from me?"

"I'm not running away." I sat in the armchair across from him. "I'm trying to understand how this could happen."

"How did you find out about Monique? What do you think you know?"

I told him about my visit with Jessie, about the journal. About how I had driven away in shock. "I didn't tell her why I was so upset. Nobody else would know about Jules and Jim. But the police will know Monique had an affair."

"Jessie stole Monique's journal?"

"Figures you would focus on that."

Johnny looked as if someone had punched him in the gut. "We were together only a short time."

He was already launching into explanations. I hadn't even asked a question. "Did you expect this to remain a secret forever? Oh, I guess it would have, if it weren't for the fire. If the Kimballs hadn't come home a few days early and then conveniently died."

"I'm sorry. I don't know what else to say."

"Were you in love with her? Are you?"

"No. I was not. I am not."

"But you slept with her."

"Yes."

"How many times?"

"I don't know—"

"Two? Three?" I'd seen movies like this, in which the betrayed wife follows her husband around the house, spearing him with desperate questions. "Ten?"

"It was short and fast . . ."

"It's clear from her letter that she was deeply in love with you."

"No, not in love," Johnny said, getting up and pacing. "Obsessed."

"You're blaming your affair on her, making her seem unstable."

"No, I'm not," he said, turning to face me. "I was on the rebound, and in a moment of weakness, there she was."

"Where did you have sex with her? Right there in the house? In our bed?"

He sat again and gripped the arm of the couch. "I knew you would ask me these questions. I'll answer them all. I told you I would. But it doesn't matter where."

"It matters to me."

"Yes."

Nausea rose in my throat. "The picture I found in the house, the woman on the dock. That's Monique, isn't it?"

"Yes."

"When was the picture taken?"

"Before I met you."

Could I believe him? "Why didn't you tell me?"

"For me, it was temporary. I didn't realize it would become something more than that for her."

"Temporary." I could sense his regret, his sadness. But I didn't care. "Did you tell her you loved her?"

"I never did. Never. I love you, Sarah."

"How do I know that?"

"I've always told you the truth. I never said I loved Monique. She understood exactly where I was coming from. I told her."

"You told her she was a temporary fling."

"Yes," he said simply. "But I didn't say 'fling.'"

"Was she already married?" I tried to keep my voice level and calm, but my words trembled with restrained fury.

"She and Chad were dating. They were serious, yes. Maybe he was serious and she wasn't. I don't know."

"The house was his, too."

"Chad bought his house about the same time I did."

"Two single men."

"He was divorced, I'd been dumped by my ex," Johnny said in a faraway voice.

"So Monique essentially cheated on him. Did you want to be with her? This beautiful French woman, every man wanted her. And you didn't? You used her for sex?"

His jaw hardened. "I didn't use her. I don't use people."

"You've been using me. Assuming you don't have to tell me the truth."

"That's not the way it is. She and I—it was mutual. We had sex. It didn't mean anything. It was casual."

"For you it was. You can just have sex. Casually." The refrigerator kicked in, a loud hum, and a wood beam creaked in the attic as the house settled.

He ran his fingers through his hair. Of course he could have casual sex. What man couldn't, in the end? What had I held on to? Assumptions as combustible as every material thing in my home? The touch of his hand at the wedding, the reciting of our vows, the way he'd so tenderly slipped the ring onto my finger, held my hand in such a tight grip. Had it all been a lie?

"I want you and you only," he said. "That is not a lie."

His words bounced off me. "I have no idea what is a lie and what is not."

"Sarah, don't do this."

"I'm not the one doing anything. You are. You did. Exactly when did it end? Were you still sleeping with her after I met you?"

He looked at his palms. "There was a short . . . overlap."

The room darkened, shadows lengthening, and suddenly there was too much furniture, too much clutter. "How much overlap?"

"I wasn't yet sure about you. You were so cautious."

"How long?"

"Not long. Nothing happened between Monique and me, not after I knew I wanted to be with you. I told you."

"She lived in the house next door. Do you think I'm some kind of idiot?" *But I am. I'm a total idiot. I couldn't see Jessie's crush on Chad, Chad's internal struggles, the fire between Johnny and Monique.*

Johnny reached out to me, but I kept my distance. His hands fell back to his sides. "You loved the house—I told you I wanted to move away. Don't you remember?"

"I do. And you did." He'd said, *Let's make a new life in a new house.* I'd said, *Why do we need to move? I love this house. I'll add my feminine touch.* "This was going on right under my nose. Why didn't I see?"

"I told you. She and I weren't meant to be together. When I saw you at the polar bear plunge, and you handed me your towel, and we started talking, I was drawn to you. We could talk about anything—literature, movies. We were comfortable together. You had the kind of beauty I couldn't stop looking at. Inside and out."

I faltered, my armor dissolving a little. "If you knew right away, why did you keep sleeping with Monique?"

"I don't know—it wasn't for long. There was something special about you. Always something new. I never felt the same way about Monique. Ever. It was casual."

"What about Mia? Is she—?"

"After I broke it off with Monique, I found out she was pregnant. I asked her if the baby was mine. I figured, if Mia was my daughter, I would do whatever Monique wanted. Marry her, even. Help her with the child."

"What did she say?"

"She said the baby was Chad's. The timing was off. I couldn't be the father."

"Did you ask her to do a paternity test?"

"Why would I? I figured she knew her own body. She knew the truth. Why would I push? Anyway, Monique made me promise to leave Mia alone, to move on. She wanted me to move away. Then the bottom fell out of the housing market. And you wanted to stay in the house."

The rain started again, pattering on the roof, the skylights. "Maybe it's in the past for you, but for me, it's new. Monique wrote about the whole thing only recently."

"Something must've happened."

"She and Chad were finally planning to move away. In her journal, she was reflecting on her relationship with you." I went to the window, rested my hand on the sill, the painted wood cool against my fingers.

"Whatever happened between Monique and me—it's in the past. I didn't lie to you. I didn't betray you."

"You don't think omission is a betrayal?" *How do we ever know about the people we love? The people we want to trust?* But if his affair with Monique had truly been in the past, perhaps, then . . . "I babysat Mia! We had drinks with Monique and Chad. We sat in the backyard, chatting about stupid things. Why didn't *she* tell me? Did you make her promise not to?"

"She did ask me about you. We did talk about how to handle the situation. She wanted to tell you. But she didn't want to destroy our marriage or hers."

"How upstanding of her. I deserved to know." I was a *situation* to be handled.

"You're right. You did, but I thought I could keep my past in the past. Now I know it's not possible."

"You should've known from the start."

"I'm sorry. What else can I say?"

"Nothing." How could I have spent so many blissful nights in our king-sized bed on Sitka Lane, my heart at ease? Certain that our happiness would last forever? "You've been getting phone calls, hang-ups. Are you having an affair now?"

He looked affronted. "What? No, of course not."

"The night of the fire, you weren't in your room. I couldn't reach you."

"I told you why."

"In light of what I now know, how can I believe you were comforting a colleague?"

"She'd lost a patient." He opened his mouth to say more, then closed it.

"If I were to talk to her, she would tell me all you did was have a drink in the bar."

"Yes, basically . . ."

"Basically?"

"That was it, Sarah. I knew her . . . before."

"Like you knew Theresa?"

"I didn't know Theresa before we moved into the cottage."

"You're not having an affair with her, either?"

"No," he said. "Her baby is not mine, either."

"But you knew this . . . colleague, before the conference."

"I knew her in medical school. She's married now. She has kids."

"Marriage isn't an obstacle for some people, apparently. They continue to do whatever they want."

"I didn't sleep with her in San Francisco."

"Then where?"

He said nothing, clasped his hands together, and looked down at them.

"In medical school?"

He didn't reply.

"I can't believe this."

"It's not what you think. She lost a patient, we had a drink, she cried into her whiskey. We went our separate ways."

I felt spent, too exhausted to ask any more questions. Was he still the Johnny I knew? The Johnny who loved me?

"What else do you want from me?" he asked in desperation, but he already knew. He got up slowly and headed for the front door, and I followed.

"Look, you can't stay here," he said. "Don't you have a book signing coming up? I saw your books at the cottage."

"I'll work it out."

"Your mom will be back soon. You're going to stay here with her?"

"I haven't thought that far ahead. I've got some things to figure out."

His expression softened, a pleading look in his eyes. "I don't want to be away from you. I've been faithful to you. I'm feeling my way through all this, just as you are. I didn't tell you about Monique because I didn't want to lose you. That's the truth. There's nobody else. Come back to the cottage. Please." He touched my cheek, his eyes full of pain.

"I need to be alone for a while, to figure things out. That's all."

"Sarah . . ."

"I need some time."

He nodded, his shoulders slumped. "I'll move into a hotel. You go back to the cottage and stay there. I'll give you the space you need. But I want you to know. I love you. I'm not going to give up. If this marriage fails, it will be because you decided to leave."

"Don't lay this responsibility on me."

"I don't mean it that way. I only mean—it will be your decision. The cottage is yours for as long as you need it." He turned and walked away, but the faint scent of him lingered in the air long after he was gone.

CHAPTER TWENTY-FIVE

When I pulled up to the cottage and found the driveway empty, my entire being went still. Johnny had drawn the curtains against an icy sky, and then he had vacated the premises. The gray morning hung lonely and desolate. The birds had gone silent, as if they sensed the chill in my soul. Even the rhododendron bushes curled their leaves against the frost.

Inside the cottage, Johnny had left the rooms pristine. His magazines were gone from the coffee table. His shoes were missing from the doormat. His coats had disappeared, the brass hooks on the wall bare, except where I'd hung my raincoat.

But his smell remained—the pine scent of his aftershave and his indefinable male aroma, reminiscent of spice and the salty sea. I'd heard that smells conjured the deepest emotional memories—it was true. I remembered the way he'd held my hand on the beach in Oahu, his impulsive stop at a roadside stand to buy me a bag of lychee fruits. He understood my moods, sensed what I needed when he made love to me. What was the measure of a marriage? These moments of caring and bliss? Or the secrets withheld?

Had I ever known the real Johnny? He was a contradiction. He became efficient under stress, and yet more absentminded in small ways. He kept track of finances but left his socks lying around. He balanced the checkbook but scattered crumbs on the countertops.

Was he still in Shadow Cove, or had he escaped to another town, where he wouldn't be easily recognized? Here in our insular community, he might run into people he knew. They would ask questions.

Had he removed his wedding ring, or did he keep it on, idly turning it around on his finger, as was his habit? He removed anything else restrictive the moment he got home. Wallet and keys, bills and coins, all emptied from his pockets.

This morning, he had taken the contents of his pockets with him. On the kitchen counter he had left me a supply of my favorite foods— soft challah bread, organic blueberries, soy milk, and ground coffee. He knew I often became so involved in writing, I sometimes forgot to eat. He wanted to remind me of his thoughtfulness. But could the good things be fairly weighed against the lies? Or more accurately, against sins of omission?

How could I concentrate on writing? My upcoming signing, at the Shadow Cove Bookstore, weighed on me. How could I smile and pretend to celebrate? I heard Natalie's voice in my mind: *Living well is the best revenge.* I would have to find a way to live well.

Or a way to simply live.

In the bedroom, the coverlet stretched across the mattress and tucked itself beneath the pillows. My normally messy husband had taken time to make the bed. Suddenly, I wanted his untidiness, the indentation in his pillow, his clothes left on a chair.

The second bedroom felt impersonal without his computer and pens, his books and mugs. The chair was locked in the reclining position, as if he had slept there. Maybe he couldn't bear the thought of climbing into bed without me. Had he slept in the hotel? Or had he merely dropped off his suitcase, brushed his teeth, and gone straight to work? Did he miss me? I wanted him to long for me, although on a deeper level, I did not want him to suffer, despite the way he had deceived me. What would bitterness accomplish?

Still, I couldn't stop dark thoughts from creeping in. How many evenings had we spent with the Kimballs, watching movies or chatting over dinner, when Johnny's arm might've brushed Monique's? When she might've leaned over him at the dining table, to place a platter of roasted vegetables on a trivet, and he might've caught a whiff of her perfume, glimpsed the curve of her breast? Made a plan for a rendezvous? Every moment carried new, adulterous meaning—the way Monique had sucked on a Popsicle on a hot day, while gazing over her sunglasses toward our backyard, where Johnny, shirtless and sweaty, had been digging in the garden.

He'd tried to leave nothing behind in the cottage. His side of the bedroom closet stood empty. He had taken all of his clothing, except for a shirt and a pair of slacks, which he'd left draped over a towel rack behind the bathroom door. For the first time since I'd known him, I found myself checking his pockets. If he hadn't insisted on taking his own suits to the dry cleaners, I might've checked his pockets before, for mundane, forgotten things. An innocent kind of search. But now I sought evidence of deception, and I found the folded receipt, in pale blue ink, with the imprint of the Harborside Florist logo at the top, for the costs of a potted hydrangea and delivery, ordered the day before Johnny and I had gone to dinner at Eris's house—paid for in cash.

I was still looking at the receipt when I heard the low rumble of a car prowling up the road. Adrian's black Buick rolled to the curb and idled in front of the cottage, and then the engine kicked off. Jessie got out of the passenger side.

I wiped my eyes, smoothed my knit sweater, and opened the front door. Unseasonably wintry air pricked at my skin. "Jessie, what's going on? Are you okay?"

"Just a minute," she shouted at Adrian. "I'll only be a minute!" She strode across the grass toward me, underdressed for the cold in a hoodie and skinny jeans. Her running shoes slipped when she reached the sidewalk, then she regained her balance and walked with her arms slightly out to the side. Her eyeliner was smudged, her face gaunt.

"What are you doing here?" I said. "You'll catch your death. Would you like a jacket? Come inside."

"I was worried about you," she said. "My mom said you and Dr. M. are getting a divorce."

"What? That's not true." The blood drained from my face. How had news of our marital trouble traveled so quickly? Who had told Pedra?

Jessie crossed her arms over her chest and glanced back toward the car, then she looked at me again, emptiness in her red-rimmed eyes. "Is it true? Are you guys splitting up? Was it the journal? He was having an affair, wasn't he? Dr. M. was banging Mrs. K."

"Banging? Who told you that?"

"I figured it out. That bites. I'm sorry."

"Jess—"

"I just came to tell you I'm leaving," she said, hugging herself around the waist now, shifting from foot to foot in the cold.

"Leaving for where? Why don't you come in? We can talk for a while. You're cold."

"I can't. Adrian wants to go right now. He has a job interview in Silverdale."

"He's not working construction anymore?"

She shook her head, kicked at the sidewalk with her shoe. "He got fired."

"What are you doing with him?" But I knew the answer. I could see it in his hulking shoulders, in Jessie's naïveté.

"I have to get out of here," she said.

"Where will you go?"

She looked up at the cottage, longing in her eyes. "We're getting a place."

"Who? You and Adrian?" This couldn't be happening. She wouldn't go with him.

She nodded toward the car. Adrian was talking on his cell phone, gesticulating. She looked at me again. "I was waiting for my birthday."

"Do your parents know?"

Adrian slammed the palm of his hand on the steering wheel. Jessie flinched perceptibly. "I left them a note," she said, looking at me with defiance.

"Think about what you're doing."

"I don't need to think. My parents don't get it. They think he's the pyro, too. They're wrong."

Was he the pyro? I wondered. "Did you return the things you took?"

"I'm going to, I promise."

Adrian got out of the car and approached us with an overconfident swagger. The air seemed to grow thin around Jessie and me, as if he sucked it all away.

"Don't go with him," I blurted to Jess. I grabbed her sleeve. She did not pull away, but she stood steadfast.

"Jess, c'mon," Adrian said, shoving his hands in his coat pockets. He came close, too close. He wore pressed khaki slacks and a wool jacket, his black shoes shiny, his hair slicked back. He towered over both of us, exuding overbearing smells of mouthwash and metallic aftershave. "We're gonna be late."

"Why don't you go to your interview and leave Jessie with me?" I said.

His dark eyes appeared oddly vacant. "Jess, come on."

The Minkowskis' house was closed and dark, both cars missing from the driveway. "Call your parents," I told Jess. "Right now. They love you. Call them."

She shook her head, looked at the ground. "I'm not going back there."

"Come with me, Jess," Adrian said.

"She's not going with you," I said. In the distance, Eris's front door squeaked open, then slammed. She clattered down the porch steps in parka and boots and strode toward us through the woods.

Adrian gazed at me as if I were merely a speed bump. "You're the writer," he said.

"I do write," I said. My heartbeat knocked around inside me.

"Stories for kids, right?" He snorted.

"They're awesome mysteries," Jessie piped up.

"But they're about a rat or something," he said. "Should I call the exterminator?"

"Mouse, actually," I said.

"Oh, a mouse. All that . . . writing about rodents. Is it why your old man left you? All the rats in your brain?" His gaze raked me up and down.

Jessie stiffened. "Adrian, come on. You don't have to insult her."

"Jess," I said. "Why don't you come inside? Let Adrian leave."

He took a hand out of his pocket and pointed his forefinger at me. "See, Jess? What did I tell you? Everyone's going to try to stop us."

Eris was halfway here, moving at a fast clip.

"Sarah, I can't stay." Jessie looked everywhere but at me.

"Let's go," Adrian said. He lunged, grabbed Jessie's arm. "We're leaving now." He dragged her toward his car.

"Stop," I said. "Stop it. Let go of her."

"Fuck off," he said. "Leave us alone."

Eris approached us, waving her cell phone in the air. "Hey!" she shouted. "Hold it right there!"

CHAPTER TWENTY-SIX

"What the hell is going on here?" Eris said when she reached me. "I'm calling the cops."

"No, don't!" Jessie said, but she had pulled away from Adrian. He did not attempt to grab her again. He stared warily at Eris.

"What are you doing to this young lady?" Eris said to Adrian.

He did not reply.

"Don't call anyone," Jessie pleaded, tugging at my sleeve. "Don't call the police. You don't need to. I'm not a minor anymore."

"But you're in danger," I said, glaring at Adrian.

"No, I'm not. Adrian and I—we just need to talk."

"Talk about what?" Eris's brows rose. "Looked like he was about to yank your arm out of the socket."

"I wasn't yanking nothin'," Adrian said. "You saw wrong. We've got ten minutes to get to my interview, babe."

"Then go," I said. "She's staying here."

"I'm moving in with him," Jess said in a shaky voice.

"Really." Eris's gaze shifted from Adrian to me and then to Jess. "Honey, he's no good for you."

Adrian burst into harsh laughter.

"You don't get it," Jessie said. "You don't understand. Nobody does."

"She wants to come with me," Adrian said. His cheeks were flushed. He held his hands slightly away from his body, his fingers curled into fists.

"She can speak for herself," Eris said smoothly. "He already hit you before, didn't he?"

Jessie went pale. "He did not hit me."

"Next time, the damage will be worse. Are you sure you want to go with this man? Think about your future."

"I am thinking," Jessie said.

"I want your boyfriend off my property," Eris said. "Right now."

I looked at her, surprised by the stony look in her eyes.

Adrian stood his ground.

"Now," Eris said. "Off."

Adrian stepped back off the curb, toward his car.

"Come on." Eris grabbed Jessie's arm and hurried her toward the wooded path. I followed.

"What if I don't want to go with you?" Jessie said, but she did not run back to Adrian.

"Believe me, honey, you want to stay with your family," Eris said, steering Jessie along. "You're lucky to have parents who give a damn about you."

"They suck," Jessie said, sniffing, but she stayed with us. Adrian got into his car and revved the engine.

"You always hate your family when you're a teenager," Eris said. "You'll realize how good you have it later on." A hint of bitterness crept into her voice.

"No, I won't," Jessie said, and she burst into tears.

Adrian screeched away from the curb, burning rubber, and raced off down the road.

CHAPTER TWENTY-SEVEN

Jessie crumpled on the porch in sobs. Eris and I tried to console her, but she had collapsed inside herself, bereft. She kept saying, "I love him I love him I love him," but I did not know to whom she was referring, Adrian or Chad—or maybe both.

Eris drove her home, and I returned to the cottage, shaky and disconcerted, Johnny's florist receipt in my pocket. I had a feeling this interlude might not be the end of Jessie's drama.

In the cottage, I could not be still. Now that Adrian knew where I was staying, alone, I no longer felt safe. But why? He had not specifically threatened me or anyone else. But still, I imagined his expressionless eyes watching me.

When Eris's car returned, she bypassed her driveway and came to the cottage. Ice pellets had begun to plummet from the sky, covering the ground in tiny, glittering shards.

"I did what I could," she said in the foyer. She looked perfectly put together, despite the weather.

"Is she all right?"

"Who knows? I tried to talk some sense into her, but there's only so much I can do. Or anyone. I was her age once. Way wilder than she is."

"She's home again?"

"For now," Eris said. She took off her gloves and placed them on the counter. "I'll make us some tea?"

A few minutes later, we sat at the breakfast nook with two mugs of tea. "Do you want to talk about it?" she said.

"She told you," I said.

"Divorce?"

"Separated for now." Outside, the ice pellets dissolved into rain.

"Was he? I mean, did he . . . ?"

"Yeah," I said.

"I'm sorry," she said in a near whisper.

"Here I am alone again, drinking tea."

"You're learning what you're made of. Haven't you heard the saying a woman is like a tea bag, you never know what she's made of until you dip her in hot water?"

"Ha ha." I laughed, holding the cup between my hands, letting the heat seep into my skin.

She reached out and rested her warm hand on my wrist. "What an asshole."

"We've been under stress. The fire burned away more than our house. It burned everything I believe in. Sorry if I sound melodramatic, but I feel dramatic. And homeless. Don't get me wrong. I appreciate the cottage. It's just that—"

"I know what you mean." She looked out the window toward the Minkowskis' house. "I understand what it's like to feel homeless. I grew up in foster homes."

"I didn't realize—"

"I didn't have a home until I made one for myself. I learned to take the reins. Nobody else would."

"You've done well," I said.

"I overcame my obstacles. I always do." She pointed two fingers at her eyes, then extended her fingers outward. "I set my sights on a goal, and I get it. Patience and persistence pay off."

"Good attitude. I admire you."

She sat back and looked down at her hands, then at me. "What do you want now that Johnny is gone?"

"Not gone for good," I said.

"The man cheated on you, and you're going to take him back?"

"No, but I mean . . . he said he didn't cheat after we were married." I sounded ridiculously lame, with the evidence in my pocket.

"I understand," Eris said. She got up, looked at her watch, then at me. "You're welcome to stay here as long as you want."

In an instant, I saw Johnny laying me on the bed, kissing my lips, my neck, lower . . . "I'm not sure," I said. "We've already made memories here."

She looked thoughtful. "I need to show you something. Wait here." She went back to her car and returned with her briefcase, from which she removed pictures of a perfect writer's retreat—a two-story cottage, ideal for one person. "It's been on the market for a while. It's a little overpriced and remote. But I could negotiate with the seller. I'm good at persuasion."

The photographs depicted a bungalow built of ecologically sustainable materials. Big bay windows overlooking the ocean. A tower room with windows in all four walls. The atmosphere in the pictures, the storybook quality of the retreat, touched a deep part of my soul. "This is stunning. But—"

"You can use the tower as a writer's studio." She pointed at a particularly magical picture of the sunset reflecting off the windows of the tower.

I felt a small spark of excitement. "But it's two hours away from here."

"True," she said. "You would be living in a whole new town, different surroundings. I could set up an appointment for tomorrow."

I looked around at the shadows and empty spaces. *Nothing is keeping me here.* "Yes," I said finally. "I would love to see the retreat."

***

My first night in the cottage alone, I dreamed of our wedding. I stood at the altar, waiting for Johnny. When I turned around, Monique blocked my way. Monique in her clinging green dress, holding her champagne glass. *Jules va bien? Quelle dommage.* I wore a white wedding gown in the dream, although in reality, I'd worn a cream-colored dress with silver lace. Johnny and I had asked our guests to donate to charity instead of bringing gifts. We'd rented the Sitka Retreat Center, on a hilltop overlooking the ocean. Nothing had gone as planned. The cake had fallen over, and the young justice of the peace, who was new to weddings, had forgotten his lines. Johnny had dropped the ring.

In the dream, I tried to push Monique out of the way. I woke up alone, to the sound of dripping rain, and everything that had happened, and what I had found, pressed in on me.

Later that morning, I rode north with Eris in her SUV, to the writer's retreat. We chatted the whole way, about real estate, the weather, ex-husbands. Eris had grown up in foster homes in California, and when she'd been emancipated, she had moved as far north as she could go before hitting Alaska.

When we finally reached the fairy-tale-like bungalow perched on a forested hillside overlooking the ocean, I thought I had found the house of my dreams, the one in which I had walked barefoot during my deepest reveries, before I'd met Johnny. Before I had fallen in love with him, I had imagined such a haven removed from civilization, awash in sunlight, replete with vaulted ceilings, hardwood floors, plush window seats, built-in bookshelves. Small enough for just me.

"Furnished," I said, walking into the living room. "Rustic couch, wow—is the house staged, or is this . . . ?"

"All the furniture is available to you," Eris said, grinning. "Top-of-the-line gourmet breakfast nook, newly remodeled. New appliances. Did you see the granite island? Amazing the architect fit it into the layout, considering the house is so small."

I pictured Mia playing in the living room in her princess night-gown, running into the kitchen for breakfast, her hair still messy from sleep. Light danced across cobalt-blue countertops, reflecting off inlaid, reclaimed glass. Blue was Mia's favorite color.

"Lovely," I said, but I hesitated, my mind pulled back to Shadow Cove. To Johnny.

"Two bedrooms, two bathrooms, another surprise in a small house. You'll never be waiting for the toilet if you have a guest."

"How did you know?" I inhaled the faint scent of new wood.

"You were talking about your dream house at dinner, remember?" Eris said, her left eyebrow rising.

"I was?"

"It was a quick comment, but I specialize in extrapolating from quick comments." Eris laughed. "We all want the same things, don't you think? A place to call home?"

"This house makes me feel hopeful again." And yet . . .

"I'm glad," Eris said, her voice buoyant. Close up, minute lines appeared next to her mouth, smudges of fatigue beneath her eyes— human touches on an otherwise flawless face. "This is exactly what you need."

"Maybe so. I'll think about it." *Or maybe Johnny and I will work things out.* But how could we?

CHAPTER TWENTY-EIGHT

In a show of support, Orla, Pedra, and Eris took me to lunch at the Shadow Café. Orla was dressed in a black turtleneck sweater and gray woolen slacks. Pedra's black satin shirt and jeans fit her tightly, the buttons threatening to pop off. She sat to my left, emitting the strong fragrance of gardenia. Eris sat next to me in an understated olive-green cotton jersey, black slacks, and black walking shoes. The three of them had already declared their allegiance to me, although I had not yet decided whether to get a divorce.

"You're sure," Orla said to me. "About the move and all."

"She's sure," Eris said, smiling. "The house is perfect. You're going to buy the place, aren't you?"

"I'm thinking about it," I said. Johnny had been calling to check on me. He wanted to come back to the cottage. I had to admit, I'd been dreaming of him, missing him.

"We're here for you," Pedra said, patting my arm. "*Díos mío.* No single person should have to deal with so much all at once. The fire, and now this—"

"They found new evidence, you know," Orla said, slicing into a salmon steak.

"Of what?" I said.

"They're not telling anyone."

"If they're not telling anyone, how do you know?" Pedra said and gulped her iced tea.

"She doesn't," Eris said.

"Lukas is a volunteer firefighter," Orla said. "Lenny isn't interested."

"You never mentioned that." I felt a sudden chill. "What does he know?"

"He doesn't know anything for sure." Orla looked at each of us in turn, narrowing her gaze, and lowered her voice to a dramatic whisper, forcing everyone to lean in toward her. "The arsonist might've set fire to the *wrong house*."

I dropped my knife on my plate with a clatter. "What do you mean, the wrong house?"

Eris laughed. "Where did you hear that?"

Pedra sat back, her face pale. "Yeah, where?"

"A trusted source," Orla said. "The fire might've been meant for another house on our block."

The blood drained from my face. "Which house?"

"No idea," Orla said. "Maybe ours."

Eris frowned. "How could an arsonist make that kind of mistake?"

"Our houses all look practically the same," Orla said.

"Oh, I don't know," Pedra cut in, looking up from her plate. "The houses have personalities."

"Can't tell the difference in the dark," Orla said. "Everything looks the same at night."

"What possible evidence could they have?" Eris said.

"I'm guessing a cell phone," Orla said.

Eris's nose crinkled. "You're only guessing?"

My heart fluttered against my ribs. Why hadn't Ryan Greene mentioned any of this? Perhaps, when he'd come to the cottage, he hadn't known.

"My son thinks he saw one in an evidence bag," Orla said.

"If you say so, but the phone could've belonged to Chad or Monique." Eris poured the dressing on her salad.

"Then it wouldn't be evidence," Orla said.

"Of course it would," Eris insisted. "But the investigators aren't going to share their findings with volunteer firefighters."

Orla gave her a sour look.

"What would be on a cell phone?" I said. I felt unsteady.

"Addresses, incriminating messages," Orla said. "Disposable phone, mind you. Untraceable."

"What kinds of messages? What addresses?" I insisted.

"Maybe the target address on the block?"

"It's all speculation," Eris said. She dug into her salad. "They didn't find any cell phone. And why are we talking about this, anyway?"

"They're analyzing evidence, most likely," Orla said. "Gas spectrometry and chromatography. I did some research on fire for a fraud case a couple of years ago. They can analyze accelerants found beneath carpets or floorboards—"

"Accelerants?" Pedra said.

"You know, gasoline or whatever fueled the fire," Orla said.

I was no longer hungry. Most of my pasta salad still sat on my plate. The smell of the smoke seemed permanently embedded in my nose.

"Doesn't every arsonist use an accelerant?" Eris said. "They spread gasoline around or throw a Molotov cocktail through a window?"

"If they find the fuel, it has its own kind of fingerprint, like DNA," Orla said, gesturing with her hands. "Sometimes they can trace it right back to the gas station where it was purchased, and they can look through the video and maybe find out who bought that particular can of gasoline."

"Whoa," Pedra said, shaking her head in wonder. "Amazing what they can do these days."

"A long shot," Eris said. "Isn't it?"

"Not at all," Orla said. "They have sophisticated forensic methods these days."

Eris's brows rose, and her lips turned down at the corners. "If that's true, I'm impressed. Maybe the arsonist is the same mentally disturbed criminal who's been setting other fires around town."

I went numb. My pasta blurred. Was Orla correct? Had the investigators found a cell phone in the rubble? Had the arsonist torched the wrong house? I needed to talk to Ryan Greene right away.

CHAPTER TWENTY-NINE

Ryan Greene ushered me into an airy office decorated with commendation plaques and photographs of three children—two young boys, one teenage girl—but no wife. I noticed, for the first time, no wedding ring on his finger. How could a man so good-looking not be married? For any number of reasons. He'd cheated on his wife, or she'd cheated on him, or he was emotionally unavailable. Or she was. Or he was gay. No, probably not. I reined in my imagination and focused on the filing cabinet with papers piled on top.

"What can I do for you?" He sat behind his desk. He looked freshly showered and shaved.

I took a seat across from him. "Mr. Greene—"

"Call me Ryan."

"I'll get right to the point. There's a rumor going around about the investigation."

"Not surprising," he said, sitting back.

"Was the fire meant for our house? Or another house on our block?"

He did not flinch or blink, and his steady breathing did not change. He rested his hands on his desk. "What makes you say that?"

"Was it?" Time slowed, dust particles hanging suspended.

"Who suggested this?"

"What does it matter? Is it true or not?"

"The investigation is ongoing," he said, tapping his fingers on the desk.

"You're not denying the rumor."

He was quiet a moment, then he said, "Do you believe your husband was where he said he was the night of the fire?"

His question slapped me in the face. I looked at the big photo on the wall, of his smiling, tanned children, and my mind went numb. "Of course I believe him. Why wouldn't I?" But I wasn't sure at all.

Ryan shrugged, unfazed by my discomfort. "Just asking."

"No, you're not. You think he had something to do with the fire."

"We're investigating every lead."

"And my husband is a lead? Is that why you can't tell me what's going on and whether or not you found a cell phone?"

"A cell phone? Is this part of the rumor?"

"Yes, that you found a cell phone as evidence."

"I can't confirm that."

"But you're not denying that you might have evidence that suggests the arsonist was trying to target another house on our block, and from your line of questioning, you think my husband might've been involved. Are you crazy?"

"I have been called crazy on occasion," he said, breaking into a smile.

"How could anyone mistake the Kimballs' house for another one on the block? The houses have identical blueprints, but they have individual personalities—"

"Arsonists make mistakes. Happened recently in Chicago, another time in Wales. One was a revenge fire, a bomb thrown from a car at the wrong house. Another one in Bend, Oregon. Kid thought he was setting fire to his ex-girlfriend's house, accidentally targeted the elderly couple next door. You take two identical houses with highly combustible cedar siding and cedar shake roofs . . . Both go up in smoke. You fill in the blanks."

"I'm filling in the blanks with 'arsonist targets the Kimballs' house for whatever reason,' and the result is tragic for them and for us." But a memory nagged at me. Once, soon after Johnny and I were married, I'd nearly turned into the Kimballs' driveway late at night but had corrected my mistake at the last moment. After that, Johnny had posted a reflective mirror at the end of the driveway, to identify our house as ours. But an arsonist would not have known. "Why would anyone want to harm someone else on our block? We're all nice people. We don't have any enemies."

"Felix Calassis seemed to think otherwise."

"What did he say?"

"Just that there was someone dangerous on your street that night. I couldn't get anything else out of him. Do you know of anyone dangerous?"

"No," I said, going numb.

"You're an author. Ever get any deranged fan mail?"

"Not really, no."

"Your husband? Disgruntled employee or patient?"

"Not that I know of."

"How is your marriage? Are you currently residing with your husband?"

A tight ball of fury rose up inside me. "What does that have to do with anything?" The air grew thick and oppressive.

"Look, if I didn't ask all the questions, I wouldn't be doing my job."

I got up, my legs shaky. "You're asking all the wrong questions."

I left in a rush, sat in the car, and took several deep breaths before driving away.

CHAPTER THIRTY

On Sitka Lane, I parked at the curb and tried to steady my nerves. A cleanup crew had scoured the two burned properties, which now appeared stark and abandoned. On the Calassises' front lawn, a rusty wheelbarrow lay on its side, spilling flowers. Next door, a large Mayflower moving van was parked in the driveway. A young, harried couple carried boxes inside the house, while two young boys played in the front yard. The **SOLD** sign had disappeared, replaced by a bicycle with training wheels, and toys were scattered across the lawn.

I got out of the car and went up to the porch to knock on the Calassises' front door. Maude answered in sweats and slippers. "Sarah, good to see you. Please come in. I heard about you and Johnny."

"We're only separated." I had called him on the drive over, to ask about the woman who had stalked him.

It's in the past, he'd said. *I miss you. I'm coming to your book signing.*

I'd hung up, perturbed. The trouble was, I missed him, too.

"I hope you two work things out." Maude let me inside and shut the door. The smell of floral air freshener mixed with a sour odor of stuffiness. A wave of nostalgia washed through me. The layout of the house felt familiar—the stairs leading up from the foyer, the hallway back to the family room. But Maude and Felix had chosen gaudy, art deco furniture; the walls were painted in Gothic shades of crimson and blue.

A boy shouted outside, and Maude flinched. "Those kids are driving me crazy. We have friends who wanted to buy that house, but . . . someone else must've made a better offer."

"That happens." Eris had not mentioned receiving competing offers for the house on the corner.

The flat drone of a television drifted from the second floor. "I wonder if I could talk to Felix," I said. "He tried to tell me something the other day."

"You can try," Maude said. "Sometimes he remembers things, but I don't know when they happened. Could've been last week or last year. He'll give you a jumble of information—real or imagined, I can't say."

"I'd like to try."

"He's upstairs. Follow me."

Maude led me upstairs into a back bedroom decorated in turquoise. Felix looked frail on the bed, reclined against numerous pillows, watching a nature show on a flat-screen TV against the opposite wall.

"Felix," Maude said, raising her voice, "you have a visitor."

He turned down the TV volume, looked up at me, and smiled. "My dear girl." He patted the bed next to him. "Come and sit."

I breathed a sigh of relief. He recognized me. I sat next to him on the soft mattress. The covers were crumpled around him, a few crumbs on his pillow, on his cheek. I rested my hand on his. "You told me to be careful. Do you remember that?"

He glanced at a heron diving across the TV screen. "Careful?"

"The night of the fire? What did you see? Were you looking through your binoculars?"

He gazed off into space. Maude lingered in the doorway. The phone rang, and she rushed back down the stairs.

"Felix," I said, taking both his cool, papery hands in mine. "I need you to talk to me. Tell me what you saw the night of the fire."

His eyes cleared a little. "I always knew that woman was trouble."

"What woman? Monique?"

"He was talking to her, arguing with her."

"Who? Who was arguing?"

He withdrew his hand, pulled at a stray strand of gray hair on top of his head. He was looking out the window, toward what? I went to the window. From here, I could see the Ramirez house, right into Jessie's room downstairs, at an angle. I could discern the outline of the dressing table. "You saw Jessie," I said. "Jessie and Adrian, maybe?"

Felix looked at me, still without understanding. "Trouble," he mumbled.

I wanted to reach in and unlock his brain, find the truth. "You saw Jessie?"

"Jessie," Felix echoed.

Footsteps creaked on the stairs. I stepped away from the window as Maude came back into the room. "Sorry about that. How's it going?" Maude looked from me to Felix and back. "Did you find out what you needed to know?"

"Not really. I'd better go." I headed for the door. "I'm afraid Felix couldn't tell me a thing."

CHAPTER THIRTY-ONE

Nobody answered the doorbell at the Ramirez house, and the driveway was empty, but I could sense someone watching me. I walked around to Jessie's room. The moss beneath the window was scuffed and flattened. She could've sneaked out, dropped to the ground, and slipped along the side of the house and down to the road. And Felix Calassis, insomniac glued to his night-vision binoculars, would've watched her, keeping her secrets. My mind raced in crazy directions. Had Jessie set fire to the Kimballs' house? Had she been jealous of Monique? Had she somehow expected Chad to survive?

"What are you doing?" a voice said nearby.

I turned to see Jessie approaching me through the grass. "Looking for you," I said.

"Why?" Jessie stiffened, suddenly guarded. She looked exhausted, her mascara smudged beneath her eyes. "I'm so *burned out.* Everything sucks."

"I'm glad you're home." She wore large hoop earrings—she'd been wearing the same earrings the night of the fire. In that moment, I realized what had been nagging at me about her. "You were already up when the fire started. You were dressed when you came over."

"Yeah, so what?" Jessie stepped back, an invisible wall going up around her.

"You changed pretty quickly. Hard to pull on those skinny jeans, isn't it? You have to lie down on the bed, hold your breath, and—"

"Are you interrogating me?"

"Did you sneak out your window that night?"

Jessie leaned on one hip, looked at her shoes, canvas Keds. The left shoe had a small rip near the toe. "They already asked me five thousand questions. The investigation is an epic fail."

"What should they be doing?"

Jessie shrugged, then looked at me through those wide, kohl-rimmed eyes. "They should be catching the guy." She traipsed around to the front porch, and I followed.

"You left through your bedroom window to meet Adrian, didn't you?"

Jessie's eyes filled with tears. "I didn't have anything to do with the fire. I swear."

"What about him? Did he have anything to do with it? Could he have . . . left something at the scene?"

"Like what? He was with me. When we got back, Adrian coasted down the road with the lights off . . . and I came home."

"You climbed back in your window."

She looked up at me with desperation in her eyes. "Don't tell anyone."

"I can't make any promises."

"Sarah, please! I didn't do anything. Adrian didn't either. I swear." Jessie bit her lip, looked down at her shoe tapping the step. "Why does everyone think Adrian is some kind of criminal?"

"Did you see anyone else out that night?"

"Nobody." Her gaze shifted to her cell phone. A text had just come through. She looked up at me. "So, you're moving away."

"What? Who told you that?"

"I heard it—some place up north?" She gave me an accusatory look.

"I saw a nice place, yes."

"You didn't want me to run away, but now you're running away."

"I'm not. I have a book signing next week, things to do here. I'm not going anywhere." This was true. I couldn't move so far away from Jessie, from Mia, from Harriet. From Natalie, when she got back.

From Johnny.

"I'll try to, like, make your book thing," Jessie said. Adrian's low-riding black Buick turned the corner, its deep bass beat thumping along the road.

"You're still with him?" I said. "He nearly yanked your arm out—"

"He didn't mean it. He's not like that."

"How can you say that?"

"I'm home, aren't I? Isn't that what everyone wanted?"

"Oh, Jessie, it's about your future."

"This is my future." The car pulled up to the curb, the engine idling. Adrian turned down the music. I had no time to ask any more questions. Jessie was already hurrying down the driveway, and I could do nothing to stop her from getting into Adrian's car with him and riding away.

CHAPTER THIRTY-TWO

I couldn't get much writing done in the cottage. I missed Johnny. The trouble was, I loved him. Love—mysterious, inexplicable, perhaps self-destructive. I felt bereft without him, like a ghost pretending to live. When I imagined spending days, months, years without him, my muscles tightened, and my head ached. I'd find myself crying at odd times—in the middle of the night, or if I spotted a rabbit in the underbrush, or a rainbow at dawn, or a deer standing motionless at the edge of the woods. I would almost go and ask Johnny to come and see, and then I would remember that he wasn't there, and my heart would sink. And the longer he stayed away, the farther from me he seemed to become.

The Minkowskis appeared to be gone. Had Theresa been an interlude, another temporary fling? When I had confronted him about his clandestine side trips to the Minkowskis' house, he'd said, *It's not what you think*. Eris kept urging me to make an offer on the writer's retreat up north. But her friend, the owner, was in no hurry to sell. And I could not bring myself to make a decision.

I had called the hotel in San Francisco. It had taken some sleuthing, but I had eventually spoken to the bartender who'd been on duty the night Johnny had met his colleague in the bar. The colleague had left without him, and Johnny had remained in the bar for a while on his own, talking to a male friend before returning to his room. Score one point for Johnny.

But still, many questions remained unanswered. Who'd been calling him and hanging up? Another woman, about whom I knew nothing?

I had almost canceled the book signing, but Eris had encouraged me to go. She'd loaned me a black Chanel sweater with a gold border. "You'll have fun," she'd said. "The signing will be a good distraction. The bookstore is lovely, too."

She was right. In an elegant blue Victorian, Shadow Cove Bookstore sat on a gentle hillside overlooking the ocean. The night of the signing, the owner, Mary Wells, greeted me at the door with her high-wattage smile.

"Are you sure you're okay to do this?" she said. She'd made flyers and posters and had arranged cookies and drinks on a table, my books displayed on another. How could I say no?

"I'm fine," I said. "Thank you for everything." Families began to show up with their children, until a dense crowd formed in the rows of chairs in front of the podium. I had not imagined so many fans in such a small town. Mary introduced me with aplomb, and I thanked her, then stepped up to speak. The room quieted. I had to survive this evening, the launch of my latest Miracle Mouse mystery, the book so crisp and new that the spine cracked a little when I opened to the first page. The smell of freshly inked paper gave me a small thrill, despite my sadness, and reminded me that I was still alive.

I spoke a little about the origins of Miracle Mouse, and then I read from the book. Miracle's adventures felt trivial, but the children loved the drama. They sat cross-legged in the front row, enraptured.

And then, Johnny arrived. He stood in the back of the audience, half in shadow. He was still in a formal shirt from work. Theresa arrived at the same time. She and Johnny stood shoulder to shoulder. She wore her hair swept up in a carefree way, as if the style was an afterthought, revealing the curve of her neck.

I faltered, then kept reading, determined to reach the end of the passage. Applause rippled through the front row of kids, and one shouted, "More!" Mia and Harriet stood off to the side, near the children's book section.

"Sarah will be signing books," Mary said, coming to the front of the crowd. "If you would like to ask any questions, now is the time."

Hands shot up in the audience. In the back, Theresa bent her head a little, turned toward Johnny. He leaned down, and she cupped her hand against his ear, whispered something. He straightened up and smiled. How could they do this? Come to my book signing together? Share secrets? Mock me?

Mary chose someone to ask a question, a white-haired man in the second row. He stood and cleared his throat. "My question is, what's your writing process?"

I smiled at him as I tried to formulate an answer. Did I even have a process anymore? "I write every morning for a few hours before other obligations intrude," I lied. I had once done so. Now I struggled. "Writing is part of who I am. Every day." Another lie.

The man nodded and sat down.

Theresa whispered to Johnny again. How could she have so much to say to him? She caught my eye and waved at me. I did not wave back. More questions followed, about where my ideas came from (I had no clue), whether Miracle Mouse was anything like me. An autobiographical mouse. Or not. Finally, Mary rescued me, taking my arm. "If you'll line up at the front, Sarah will sign books now."

"I have to make a pit stop," I said to her. I could no longer see Johnny through the throng. I dashed to the bathroom, but Harriet stopped me. Her face looked pale and drawn. Mia stood next to her, eyes wide, gripping her grandmother's hand.

"Mia, Harriet! Thank you for coming," I said, realizing I should have said hello to them earlier. I reached down and hugged Mia. "How is my little princess?"

"I'm fine, thank you." Mia was unnaturally polite, perhaps subdued by all the people. "Am I going to your house?"

"I don't know—what does your grandma say?"

"Grandma says we're going home for now," Harriet said.

I touched her arm. "How are you? I left you a few messages."

"I meant to call you back, but I've been preoccupied," Harriet said. "I have to go in overnight again."

"Harriet, oh, my goodness."

"Could you take Mia? I know it's short notice."

A man jostled me as he passed. "Certainly, of course. I would be happy to . . . But when?" I would have to do this one alone.

Mia tugged at her grandmother's arm. "I want to go to Auntie Sarah's house. She has a donut swing."

"You can come back anytime," I said.

"Thank you, Sarah." Harriet gave me a grateful smile.

Somebody was calling for me, and Mia and Harriet disappeared in the crowd. I rushed to the bathroom, locked myself inside, splashed cold water on my face. I couldn't go back out there, couldn't face all those people. But there was no other exit from the bathroom.

I had no choice. I had to sign books. When I opened the door, Johnny stood in front of me. He had the haggard look of a troubled, haunted man. He took me in his arms, held me tight. "I've missed you," he said.

"I've missed you, too." It was the truth. But my body could not relax against him.

"I want to come home."

"Home? You mean the cottage?"

"Wherever. Home is with you."

"I'm not ready. What about Theresa?" I pulled away, my body stiffening.

"I need to show you something. I wanted to do this earlier, but the Minkowskis were away."

"I have to sign books."

"That's okay," Johnny said, taking my hand and leading me back out into the crowd. "I'll wait."

CHAPTER THIRTY-THREE

Johnny followed me back to the cottage in his RAV4, parked behind my car, and walked me over to the Minkowskis' house. A soft rain pattered down in the darkness.

"What are we doing here?" I said.

He took my hand. "You wanted to know what's been going on. I'm going to show you."

"So, you *have* been coming here to see Theresa."

"Give me a chance." He looked at me with that clear-eyed, sincere gaze. "I was going to wait, but now, considering you and I are not even sleeping under the same roof, I have to show you."

"What do you mean, show me?"

"Bear with me." He steered me up the steps and in through the front door. Theresa must've known we were coming. I smelled chemicals again, and perfume.

"Kadin's out with his dad," Johnny said.

"Hey, Sarah," Theresa said, coming down the hall. She looked stunning with her hair swept up.

"What's going on?" I said, a bitter taste on my tongue.

"Come on back. I want to show you something."

Johnny let go of my hand and ushered me forward, ahead of him.

I followed Theresa down the hall, and into a spacious room in the back. Johnny stayed right behind me. The lights were dim, large windows facing the backyard. The room was lined with shelves and supplies—bottles of cleaners, chemicals, lacquer, oils. Brushes and glues. There were two long worktables with myriad pieces of artwork and ceramics in various states of disrepair or repair, depending on one's viewpoint.

There was an easel covered in burlap. Theresa walked into the center of the room. Then she spread her arms and took a deep breath. "This is it, my home workshop." She and Johnny traded another knowing look. I pictured him veering off the main trail in the woods, heading here to rendezvous with Theresa.

Johnny gave her a subtle nod, and she lifted the canvas cover and flipped it back over the easel. The cover fluttered to the ground. The smell of paint grew stronger. She stepped aside to reveal a painting I had never expected to see again. I gasped, unable to speak.

"This is what I've been working on, when I have time," Theresa said. "Johnny brought it over after the fire."

I stared at Miracle Mouse, the painting partly restored. No frame. A gray film of soot still covered the bottom third, the paint darkened as if a permanent diagonal shadow had fallen over the canvas. But the darkness gave way to light. The top two-thirds of the painting looked new, replenished, vibrant.

I moved in slow motion toward the picture, reached out, pulled back my hand. The paint was still wet. This was Miracle Mouse, her whiskers alive, almost twitching. Miracle with her shiny spectacles, her erudite eyes. One ear flopping forward, the round glasses slipping down her nose.

I turned to Johnny, my eyes full of tears. "When did you find this? How did the painting survive?"

"It was the only thing in your study that wasn't completely burned. A miracle."

"Yes," I whispered.

"It was blackened and warped," Theresa said. "The canvas was cracked. The painting was badly fire-damaged. When Johnny brought it to me, he wasn't sure if it was salvageable, and neither was I. But I told him I would try to save it. He said it meant a lot to you."

Tears slipped down my cheeks. "Thank you—yes. My grandmother painted it. I thought . . . I thought Miracle Mouse was gone."

"I can brighten the rest of the painting, but it's going to take a while," Theresa said. "We were going to give it to you by your birthday in December."

"But you kept following me over here," Johnny said. "I came to check on the progress of Theresa's work, but then you decided to be a sleuth."

What was I seeing? A glimmer of our former life, like a single ray of sunlight in the darkness. "I . . . didn't realize. Theresa, thank you. You can work miracles."

"I can't. But I try. Not everything can be saved," she said. "Miracle will never be entirely new again, but I can bring her pretty damned close."

"Restoration is her specialty," Johnny said. "I was going to give it to you good as new, but as you see, it's not done."

"This is why you were coming over here," I said.

He nodded, and Theresa looked down at her shoes. "When you started asking me questions, I had to think fast," he said. "I kept compounding my lies. I'm not used to doing that. I'm not perfect, but I'm not a liar."

I wiped away my tears. "I'm almost disappointed that it's not going to be a surprise."

"We held off as long as we could," Theresa said, smiling at Johnny. He shrugged, looked at the floor.

We all went back to the front door, and Johnny walked me back to the cottage.

"When can we resolve this?" he said. "I want to be with you."

I looked into his eyes, not sure what I saw there. He looked so sincere, regretful. "I believe you, and what you did . . . it's beautiful and thoughtful."

He stepped closer. "I don't want you away from me. I can't sleep. I can't eat."

Neither can I. "I need a little more time. To process everything."

"Is there a chance for us?" he said.

I hesitated a moment, then said, "Yes, there is a chance."

He breathed a deep sigh of relief, his whole body relaxing. "Good." He touched my cheek gently, and as he turned and headed for his car, Ryan Greene drove up and parked. When he got out, his face was grim. He appeared to have been interrupted in the middle of a workout. He wore running shoes and a jogging suit that conformed to his tall, muscular frame, his hair windswept and damp.

I instantly tightened, wanting to turn and stride away from him. If he planned to interrogate me again, I would have none of it.

"Thought you'd like to know," Ryan said. "We believe we've identified the arsonist."

CHAPTER THIRTY-FOUR

Shadow Cove Register

Arsonist suspect found dead of an overdose

Forty-year-old Todd Severson was found dead in his Olalla home today of an apparent overdose of methamphetamine, according to police, although further details will not be released before an autopsy can be performed. Mr. Severson was a person of interest in the arson investigation into the deaths of two Shadow Cove residents last month and the destruction of two homes in a fire on Sitka Lane, in addition to other unsolved arson cases in the county.

"We cannot draw conclusions at this time," said Fire Marshal Ryan Greene of the Shadow Cove

Fire Department. According to Severson's neighbors, he was a quiet man who kept to himself and ran Severson Home Repair and Remodeling, helping various residents with projects around town. He was also a volunteer firefighter.

"You never would've known he was into drugs," said neighbor Kathy McClinnon, forty-nine. "Course, after his wife left, he kept to himself more. Worked a lot more."

Severson's estranged wife declined to comment . . .

Eris put down the newspaper and shook her head. "I can't believe he was the arsonist. I had him coming to your cottage—and working on other properties."

"You couldn't have known," I said, sitting at the table in Eris's kitchen. The scent of blueberry muffins wafted from the oven. Todd had warned me about crazy people in Shadow Cove. He'd been referring to himself. *Nobody was supposed to die.*

"What if he'd lit a match when one of us wasn't home?" Eris went on. "The man was a pyromaniac. I thought I knew him."

"He seemed regretful," I said. "Maybe he thought the houses would be empty."

"Why would he think such a thing?"

"Maybe he'd been watching the Kimballs' house while they were away, and he didn't expect them to come home early."

"We can't know what was going through his mind," Eris said.

"They found methamphetamine at his place. But he didn't seem like an addict."

"Nobody ever seems like it." Eris wiped the counter, put a carton of milk back in the fridge.

I gazed out through the trees toward the cottage, clearly visible from here.

"He was a firefighter. I still don't understand how he could do this."

"Did you ever see that movie *Backdraft*? The arsonist was a fire-fighter in that one, too. They're drawn to fire. They set one, and then they get to return to the scene of the crime and become all heroic dousing the flames. A double whammy."

"Not all firefighters are like that," I said.

"Nope, but you get your one bad seed—"

"He did seem remorseful."

Eris shrugged. "Speaking of remorse, what about that husband of yours?"

"I've been too hard on him."

"You'll find someone better."

"He's flawed. But aren't we all?"

"Some of us are more flawed than others." Eris took a plate of butter out of the fridge, then busied herself loading dishes from the sink into the dishwasher.

"It wasn't all a lie. I mean, he hurt me, but I believe he loves me. He wishes he'd told me about Monique."

"I'll bet he does." Eris turned off the oven, brought out a tray of muffins, and set them on the stovetop to cool.

Tears pushed at the backs of my eyes.

Eris came and sat next to me, rested a hand on mine. "I felt sad about my ex, too. But I survived. So will you. You've got your friends, your writing. You are strong."

I nodded, still bereft. "He was having a painting restored for me. He's a good man."

"Of course." Eris nodded sympathetically. She got up and took a tub of yogurt from the fridge. "Smoothie to perk you up?"

"Thank you." I needed to talk to Natalie, but I would have to wait. She was en route back home.

Eris threw yogurt in the blender. Then she chopped up bananas and turned on the blender. The grating noise jarred my eardrums, but the resulting smoothie tasted heavenly. "You're an expert at this," I said. "I feel better already."

She sat next to me again and grinned. "My smoothies are the Rx for grief. Your life is going to get better."

"I hope so." I gazed into my half-empty—or half-full—glass, but the smoothie gave up no secrets. "I'm going to take a leap. I'm going to try again with Johnny."

Eris regarded me with curiosity and concern. "You think he can change?"

I sipped the last of the smoothie, letting the cool, thick liquid slide down my throat. "He can't change what he did before he met me."

Eris nodded thoughtfully. "Like I said, I got a little wild when I was young. But I got over it. I matured. I wouldn't want anyone judging me for my past, either."

"That's what I mean." I finished off the smoothie.

I turned the empty glass around in my hand. Afternoon sun cast a ray of almost-white illumination across the tile floor. A play of light and leaves danced across the wall above the sink.

"I understand," Eris said, and got up. "But you may regret it later."

CHAPTER THIRTY-FIVE

"Where's Uncle Johnny?" Mia said as she skipped into the cottage, holding Princess Barbie. She wore a new pair of sparkling princess shoes. The afternoon hung gray and humid, the sky brooding, warning of a coming storm.

"He's away," I said. "He's in Seattle."

"See-at-ul," Mia said, jumping up and down in the foyer. "When is he coming back?"

"Late." But he was coming. He was to move back in that evening. I'd been a mess of anticipation, unable to concentrate.

On the drive back from the hospital, where I'd left Harriet, I'd stolen glances at Mia, trying to detect any resemblance to Johnny. What about Mia's double-jointed thumbs, the way she stuck out her tongue? Could any of these traits come from him?

No, I'd concluded, as I'd hauled Mia's heavy overnight bag into the cottage. Her chin had a slight cleft, exactly like Chad's.

"I want Uncle Johnny to read to me," Mia insisted, stamping her foot on the floor. "*Goodnight Moon.*"

"You *are* a little princess, aren't you?"

"Uncle Johnny." Mia pouted halfheartedly, pulling a new set of Dr. Seuss books from the bag. No wonder the darned thing was so heavy.

"He's teaching a class at the university. He might be late." He'd been invited to give a guest lecture on general pediatric dermatology. I'd barely had a chance to talk to him in the past week, except to tell him I was ready to sit down with him, to discuss the future. His voice had become buoyant and hopeful. *As soon as I get back,* he'd said.

Tonight, tonight, tonight . . . Wasn't that a song?

I missed the sound of his voice, the way he left newspapers strewn on the table, crumbs under his chair. His special interest in cooking Indian food. The way he often read aloud to me before bed. The way he took his time touching me, as if he had nowhere else to go and nothing else to do for the rest of his life. The cottage felt strangely large and empty without him.

The Minkowskis were gone, their house locked up, the blinds drawn. They had flown to Florida, as Kadin's father had suddenly passed away. The painting of Miracle Mouse remained in Theresa's studio, waiting for her to finish the restoration. Eris was home but often out at meetings or making lucrative real estate deals.

Mia's nonstop chatter offered a pleasant distraction. She never tired of finding new ways to play. She helped me bake an elaborate cake, creating a mess of flour all over the kitchen.

Finally, she collapsed on the cot for her afternoon nap. Her chest rose and fell in an easy rhythm, her face peaceful. In the soft lamplight, she resembled a young Monique. Apparently, she'd begun to act out, to remember her fear during the fire. She woke crying in the night. But I had not seen any evidence of her sadness since she had arrived at the cottage.

I sat on the couch to write on my laptop, grateful for Mia's company. Her grandmother probably appreciated having her around, too. Harriet had appeared frailer than usual that morning. She'd mentioned her sister in Vermont. *She'll fly in if I need her.* Didn't Harriet need her now?

She was alone at the hospital. Mia and I had stayed there awhile, but Mia had grown restless, so I'd brought her home. We would go back to see Harriet later. I'd left my number with the nurse.

Mia had been napping for barely fifteen minutes when my cell phone lit up. My heart leaped. *Johnny.* Maybe he'd finished his lecture early. But it wasn't him. It was Jessie.

"Can you come and get me?" Her voice was high-pitched and tearful.

I replied in a low voice. "Mia's asleep. What's wrong? Are you with Adrian?"

"No. I'm walking to your house. Can you pick me up?"

"Walking to my house from where?"

"I'm on Cedar Drive but I have, like, two more miles to go, and it's raining."

"I can't leave Mia alone. Can you call your parents? What's going on?"

"Sarah, please. I can't call them." Jessie broke into hiccupping sobs.

"Are you okay? Do you need to hang up and call 911?"

"No, I—I need you."

"Can you take a cab home?"

"I took a cab here, but I ran out of money."

"Keep walking on Cedar. I'll find you."

I called Eris to come and watch Mia, and a few minutes later, Eris showed up at the door in jeans and a rain jacket, shaking her umbrella. She took off muddy boots. "Where's the kid?" she whispered. She looked pale, dark circles under her eyes.

"Are you okay?" I asked.

"Fine." But she didn't look fine. Perhaps she'd fought with her boyfriend. He hadn't come around in a few days.

"She's in the bedroom." I showed her Mia asleep on the cot. "I'll be right back."

"I'll take good care of her," Eris said.

"Thank you for watching her." I grabbed my keys and purse. "I don't know what happened to Jessie, but it sounds bad."

"Did you call her parents?" Eris whispered back.

"I left a message for her mother."

"Go on then, hurry." Eris waved me away.

I drove slowly along Cedar Drive, scanning the sidewalks through sheets of rain. Finally, I spotted a hunched figure. I pulled over and opened the passenger side door. Jessie got in, a waterlogged waif in a hoodie, soaked to the skin. Her hands trembled as she dropped her wet backpack on the seat. I reached over her and shut the door. She smelled of clove cigarettes and wet wool.

"Put on your seat belt," I said.

Jessie clipped on her seat belt with shaking fingers.

I pulled back into the road, made a U-turn.

Jessie looked at me from beneath her hoodie, her face shadowed. "Where are we going?"

"I'm taking you home."

"I thought we were going to your house."

"We can't go to my house. You need to talk to your parents."

"But I can't." She covered her face with her hands, her shoulders shaking.

"Why not?"

"This is why not." She pulled off her hoodie, revealing her face, the black bruise on her cheek, her swollen eye, her split and bloody lip.

I gasped and nearly swerved into the ditch. "I'll kill that asshole."

Jessie said nothing, her lips trembling.

"I'm taking you to the hospital," I said.

"No, Sarah, please."

"Don't argue with me."

"My parents will find out."

"We'll make it through this, okay?" I headed straight for Cove Hospital, my fingers gripping the steering wheel. I resisted cursing aloud. "You need to press charges."

Jessie wiped her nose with the palm of her hand. "I hate myself."

"Don't say that. Don't you ever say that."

"I'm so stupid."

"You are not stupid. Where is he? You need to call the police."

"I don't want to. I don't know how he knew."

"About what?"

"Chad. Someone told him."

"Oh, Jessie. How could anyone else know? Maybe he guessed."

"I don't want to go to the hospital."

"You need stitches." I pulled into the parking lot at Cove Hospital. "Come on. Let's go in."

I got out, dialing Pedra as rain pelted my skin. I led Jessie inside the hospital, into the emergency room. "*Díos mio*," Pedra said into the phone. "I'll be right there."

Next, I called Eris. She gasped, cursed under her breath. "You're kidding. Keep me posted."

Ten minutes later, Pedra rushed into the waiting room, Don in tow. They were both white-faced. "Jessie, what happened?" Pedra took Jessie's face in her hands.

Tears spilled down Jessie's cheeks.

I pulled Don aside. "I have to go. I'm babysitting Mia. I left her with a neighbor."

He nodded, his eyes bewildered and angry. I worried about what he might say to Jessie, whether he would blame her. But I had to get back. I hugged Jessie, squeezed her hand, then called Eris again on my way back to the car.

"Is Mia awake yet?"

"She got up. We're playing." Her voice sounded crackly and distant, as if she had turned on the speakerphone. "You're on your way back?"

"I'll be there in ten minutes."

When I got back, the cottage was dark and quiet, save for the soft hum of the refrigerator and the fan of my laptop computer, which I'd left turned on in my hurry. No sign of Mia or Eris. Mia must've woken up. Eris must've taken her next door. I dialed Eris's cell, but the call went straight to voice mail.

In the master bedroom, my journal sat on the bed. The journal in which I had meticulously documented everything that had happened after the fire, every thought and emotion. I didn't remember leaving the journal on the bed, but I must have.

Still in my raincoat and boots, I rushed outside and took the wooded trail to Eris's house. I knocked on the front door, but nobody answered.

I tried calling Eris's cell phone again. Voice mail. Eris's car still sat in the driveway—but the house was dark. I followed a worn path around to the back, peered in the windows. No sign of anyone. Nobody answered the side door to the kitchen. The door was unlocked, so I went inside. "Eris! Mia!" I called out. A plate sat on the counter, sprinkled with toast crumbs, next to a coffee cup and a teaspoon. In the dining room, the air smelled of orange polish.

"Eris! Mia!" No answer. Soft classical music drifted down from the second floor. "Eris! Mia!" Still no answer.

I followed the source of the music upstairs to Eris's quiet room. A soft Brandenburg concerto played inside. I knocked, but nobody answered. I turned the knob, and to my surprise, the door opened easily. "You guys in here?" I called into the dimness. A single window cast diffuse light on a crumpled bedspread and outlined the shapes of a dresser, chair, and bookshelf. Maybe Eris had brought Mia in here to calm her down. But again, nobody answered.

The air hung heavy with incense and perfume. I flipped a switch on the wall next to the door, and a line of track lights flickered on overhead. I gasped and nearly stumbled backward. The concerto played on, an incongruous accompaniment to the unbelievable scene now in front of me. Nobody was in here, but Eris had turned the room into a shrine, a temple, but not in tribute to any god—in this room, Eris worshipped Johnny.

CHAPTER THIRTY-SIX

I stepped farther into the room, my breathing fast and shallow, my heartbeat a rapid gallop. What kind of sick obsession was this? This perfumed room made into an elaborate shrine to Johnny? His face stared out from photographs plastered on the dresser mirror, framed behind glass on the walls.

That's my quiet room.

In the open closet, silk negligees hung in a rainbow of colors—red, violet, turquoise. Spaghetti straps and lace, stiletto heels and G-strings, cologne bottles lined up on the dresser. Lotions, makeup, hairbrushes. Condoms, still in their colorful wrappers, arranged on a plate, like finger foods at a party.

What about the bed pressed against the window, the blankets in a tangled mess? Did Eris sleep here every night, on that single pillow, gazing at the photographs of Johnny? Was this her bedroom? Who could live in a space like this one, full of crazy longing and fixation?

A bottle of wine sat on the nightstand next to two glasses. Untouched glasses, waiting for a man who might never come, and it wasn't just any bottle of wine. It was the bottle of Chardonnay that Johnny had given to Eris. Unopened. She had not offered to open the bottle during dinner. She had spirited the bottle away, had returned with raspberry wine.

On a bookshelf, medical textbooks were arranged alphabetically by title, some still wrapped in plastic—Eris had bought them but never bothered to open them. And architecture magazines. Self-help books. *How to Snag Him and Keep Him. Your Lovable Self. Perfect Skin.* Who read books like this? I started to hyperventilate, nausea rising in my throat.

Breathe. Think. What's going on here? A large pair of binoculars sat on the windowsill. Eris had a perfect view of the cottage from here—a direct line down the path through the woods. She could not possibly see into the rooms from this distance. But she could watch Johnny and me coming and going. She could slip inside the cottage when we weren't home, with an extra key.

She had taped photographs around the perimeter of the dresser mirror. Johnny mid-stride, coming out of the clinic in his suit. Johnny sitting in the RAV4. Johnny jogging up the trail. Johnny emerging from the house on Sitka Lane, getting into his car. Eris must've used a telephoto lens. She'd added Johnny to photographs of herself, and she had removed other people from the pictures. Eris and Johnny in a swimming pool, on a ski slope, gazing at each other over a candlelit table. The picture of Johnny on the dock. Eris must've stolen it from the cottage. She'd cut Monique out of the photograph.

I trembled all over. This couldn't be real. Draped over a chair were three polar bear plunge T-shirts, all in Eris's size, but otherwise identical to Johnny's shirts. Had she gone looking for them? Had she ever worn them?

She had arranged a circle of candles on the dresser, a handwritten note in the center, next to a cutout picture of Johnny's face. *The time will come, my love,* the note said. *Until then.*

I was noticeably absent from all of the pictures. No photograph of me with my face slashed, no mug shot with a dart in my forehead. No, to Eris, I simply didn't exist. If I'd been in any of the photographs with Johnny, I had been summarily deleted.

How could Eris project such a confident, normal, self-assured exterior? Such friendliness? When she had claimed to be in love, she hadn't been talking about Steve. She'd been referring to Johnny, the man she thought was stuck in an unhappy marriage, waiting for freedom from "entanglements." There were two Erises, the one in here and the one out there. The one in here frightened me to death.

The one out there had Mia.

CHAPTER THIRTY-SEVEN

I raced out of the room, the music receding behind me as I stumbled down the stairs, punched 911 into my cell phone, yelled that a deranged neighbor had kidnapped Mia Kimball and to come right away. I left a message for Johnny. "Hurry, come back. Eris is crazy. She has Mia. She's taken her somewhere." Next I left a message for Ryan Greene, and I ran outside into the wind, down the driveway to the street, screaming for Mia. Where could Eris have possibly taken her?

To the river.

At the entrance to the trail, Mia's pink hair ribbon dangled from a branch, as if Eris had deliberately put it there to lure me. The rain had stopped for the moment, but a new, destructive autumn storm brewed in black clouds. I'd left Mia with a psychopath. How could I have messed up so badly?

As I ran down the muddy trail, I began to cry, yelling for Mia, but nobody answered. The rain came down in a sudden squall, forming narrow rivulets on the trail, slipping inside my raincoat. My shoes became instantly waterlogged. I could hear myself yelling for Mia, my voice carried away on the wind. I finally spotted Eris in her yellow raincoat, poised at the high riverbank, holding on to a much smaller, whimpering person.

"Mia!" I shouted, running toward them. "Eris, let her go!"

"Don't come one step closer," Eris yelled. She yanked Mia closer to the cliff. The wind picked up, whipping the trees. A branch snapped across the river, crashed into the water.

"Don't you dare hurt her!" I shouted, shivering. "Get away from the edge!"

"Or what? Stay where you are." Eris stepped closer to the embankment. Clods of soil tumbled down into the river.

"Give Mia back to me."

Mia cried, and Eris yanked her arm, nearly pulling it out of the socket. "Shut up, you little bitch."

Mia fell silent.

"Let her go," I said again, trying to keep calm. "Mia, everything is going to be okay."

"Auntie Sarah!"

"Don't talk to her," Eris said.

"What do you want?" I said.

"You know what I want."

"No, I don't. Tell me."

"You should've died in the fire. Then none of this would be necessary."

You should've died. The words blew through me with hurricane force. "Let her go. Mia, it's okay. I'm here. Auntie Sarah is here. Eris, just tell me what you want."

"That idiot didn't know what he was doing. He set fire to the wrong damned house. They all look the same in that neighborhood. So I've had to fix everything."

"You sent Todd to set fire to our house."

"The man was an idiot pyromaniac with a drug habit. He didn't know where to stop."

Todd Severson. He'd been working for Eris all the time—fixing flushes and setting fires. "Don't involve Mia," I said. "Give her to me." What if the police didn't see the ribbon on the branch? What if they didn't know where to go? I took out my cell phone.

"Make a call, and Mia goes in the river," Eris said.

"Mommy!" Mia cried.

"Shut up," Eris said.

"She has nothing to do with this," I said.

"I went to him, you know," Eris said in a childish voice. "But he doesn't get it yet."

"You went to whom? Johnny? When?"

"I gave him the time he needed. He finally escaped from you. So I went to see him. But he wasn't ready."

"What do you mean?" I inched forward, tried to gauge the distance between me and Eris. If I lunged, Eris would still have time to throw Mia into the river.

"Hold still," Eris said. "You're always trying something. Why didn't I do the job myself? Because I'm nice. I give people the benefit of the doubt. After the fire, I had second thoughts. Two innocent people died. That was not my intention. This poor little girl suffered. Everyone suffered. *Johnny suffered.* I never wanted him to experience a moment of pain."

"He'll be in more pain if you hurt Mia." My teeth chattered. Mia whimpered.

"No, he won't. He doesn't want her."

"Yes, he does."

"I thought, since Todd made such a mess of things, I would take a more compassionate route. Then I thought, maybe he didn't make such a bad mistake, after all. I read your journal, about Johnny's affair. Monique deserved to die."

"No, she didn't." I'd written so much in that new journal . . . Had Eris read everything?

"I read about Jessie's crush on Chad, such a sordid business. I thought her lovely boyfriend, Adrian, ought to know. Don't you think?"

"You told him?"

"I take my responsibilities very seriously."

"Do you have any idea what you've done? He could've killed her."

"Oh, he would have done that all by himself, eventually. Jessie and Adrian, they were easy. You're the difficult one. I tried to make you see, *you are not the right woman for Johnny.* But it wasn't enough for you, all the *evidence I threw right in your face.*"

"What evidence?"

"Theresa. The receipt for the flowers."

"You put the receipt in the cottage." I inched forward again, a little at a time.

"I gave you so many chances. I showed you the perfect little writer's retreat, nice and far away."

"You told everyone Johnny and I were divorcing."

"You didn't buy the retreat. You're an idiot."

I took another step forward. "Let's talk about this somewhere warm and dry—"

"Shut up!" Eris teetered close to the edge, slipping a little. Mia screamed. A few rocks tumbled into the rushing river. "You're blind. What would it take? You just. Would. Not. Leave."

"I see it all now," I said. "You and Johnny are meant to be together. I'll leave, but you have to give Mia to me."

"You think I'm stupid? You babbled on about how much you miss him. Then you wrote all your melodrama in your journal. You decided you still love your husband. Blah blah blah."

I struggled to see the Eris I thought I knew—the confident, helpful Realtor. My friend. "Let her come to me. I'll give you whatever you want."

"What I want is not yours to give. You've always been in the *fucking way.* Johnny and I—the moment we met, I knew. All the signs were there. At my last follow-up appointment, we talked about everything. Real estate, art and architecture, our dreams. You don't even know how to talk to him. You don't share any of his interests. You *beguiled him* into marrying you."

"Takes two to tango." One more step and I could get close enough to grab Mia. Eris practically dangled her over the edge.

"I don't get it. You in your frumpy clothes, clueless. But you've still got him under your spell. Did you threaten him?"

"What about Steve?"

"He's my divorce attorney, you idiot."

His frown, his brusque manner. It made sense now. "I'm taking Mia home," I said. A crackle of lightning flashed overhead, a jagged line across the clouds—and a moment later, the crash of thunder. Mia burst into tears.

"Auntie Sarah. Mommy! Auntie Mommy!"

To hell with Eris. I raced forward, too late. Another lightning bolt split the sky as Eris shoved Mia down the embankment, sending her screaming and sliding down the steep slope.

"Mia! Grab on to a branch. Grab on!" I called. But Mia kept tumbling down, seemingly in slow motion, her little hands grasping on to shrubs, protruding branches, but slipping away, finding nothing to hold on to as she fell into the river.

"Mia!" I ran back and forth along the cliff, found an opening, and slid down on my rump, my hands scraping against jagged rocks. "Hang on, honey, I'm coming."

But the current had already captured Mia, carrying her away. I glanced up toward the cliff, but I could see no sign of Eris. The embankment was too steep here; I could no longer even slide down. I had to fall, or dive, into the water. I had no choice. I held my breath and plunged into the icy depths of the black, rushing river.

CHAPTER THIRTY-EIGHT

I'm drowning.

The river's current is tearing me apart. I've lost sight of Mia. What if she's already dead? The driving rain blocks my view. Now and then, I glimpse shadowy trees swaying on the distant shoreline. But not her.

She's gone—no, there, her head bobs to the surface, her face upturned. *No, not yet.* I strike out after her, cutting through black water, but the current yanks me down; I swallow mouthfuls of water as I sink. My lungs fill with muddy liquid, but I fight my way upward. My lungs will explode, I can't take any more, but now I break the surface, sucking in the cold air. I spit out sand and silt, the metallic taste of ice melt from the mountains. I hear it, the roar of the waterfall. I won't reach her in time. She'll hurtle over the edge, plummet to the rocks below. And I will follow, both of us battered and broken. There she is again, her face white against the darkness.

"Mia!" I cry. "Grab on to something!" But the roaring river absorbs my voice. It can't end like this. I saved her once. I can save her again.

My mind sharpens, suddenly aware of the forest, a dragonfly flitting in an arc over the river, a towhee flying near the shore. Part of my brain remains calm. *Don't panic.* Pilots don't panic when their planes flip upside down. Astronauts don't panic if they run out of air. They work to correct the problem. Panic does not save lives. And what about cave divers? Those brave souls who don scuba gear and descend hundreds of feet into those caverns filled with water, created over thousands of years? They pull nylon lines with them, hold on to the lines even when debris fills their field of vision, so they don't know which way is up. They hold on, and by holding on, they survive.

These thoughts race through my mind in an instant, outside of time. I'm catching up to Mia. She floats facedown, her mermaid hair splayed out in the water. Her head bobs under, resurfaces. In one superhuman, final push, I reach her, grab her, and turn her over. Her eyes are closed, her face pale and serene, her lips blue.

"Stay with me," I say, pulling her toward the shore. I'm losing strength. The water is too cold. The current drags me under again, and I almost let go of Mia. She floats like a rag doll.

A dark figure emerges high on the embankment. Eris. She follows us along the cliff toward the waterfall. The noise of the water grows louder, deafening now. Eris's silhouette, high on the shoreline, wavers in the rain. We are dead, Mia and I—perhaps we've been doomed from the start. As I sink, a light appears in the sky, through the mirage of water.

My muscles turn to liquid. I can't breathe, can't hold on. Mia slips from my grasp.

"Sarah!" someone calls out. Sounds like Johnny. But how could he be here? I'm imagining his voice, his hand reaching down from the heavens to pull me to shore.

CHAPTER THIRTY-NINE

Boxes, piled in the cottage foyer.

After so little time here, Johnny and I have accumulated too many belongings. Perhaps it's human nature to cling to the material world, to remind ourselves we're alive. Still, I've learned to make do with fewer possessions, to cherish the beauty of moments. The rising sun on this clear winter morning; resident towhees flitting through the underbrush; the distant blare of the ferry foghorn as the boat glides into the harbor. But I could do without the rush of the river. In my nightmares, I'm still swallowing water, still reaching for Mia as she slips away.

Ryan Greene rescued her just in time. He brought medics with him, and the police arrested Eris. But it was Johnny who pulled me to safety. Johnny, my guardian angel.

He carries a box of dishes from the kitchen straight out to the trunk of his car. He returns in long, confident strides, although his hair is still rumpled from sleep. "Almost full," he says.

"Good thing we're almost done." I pick up a box of clothes, but he stops me.

"You're not supposed to lift anything," he says.

"I'm fine." But my lungs still ache a little. The doctor wanted to keep me in the hospital a second night, but I had to get out. I've had more than my share of hospital stays.

"I'll do it." He balances two boxes of clothes in his arms, but puts them back down when Ryan Greene arrives in his truck. He gets out looking like a weekend lumberjack in scuffed jeans, plaid shirt, and boots.

"Morning," he says. "Moving day?"

"Can't come too soon," I say.

"Where you folks going?"

"Rental uptown," Johnny says, shaking hands with Ryan.

"Until we figure out what to do," I add.

Ryan nods, looks at his shoes, then up at me. "I just stopped by Sitka Lane, saw your neighbor, Felix Calassis."

"How is he?"

"He saw Eris Coghlan the night of the fire, arguing with Todd Severson."

That woman is trouble. "I thought he saw Jessie sneaking out. He meant he saw Eris."

"Not sure he knows what he saw," Ryan says. He pulls something from his back jeans pocket and hands it to me. A folded page covered in handwriting. *My* handwriting. My deepest emotions laid bare. The pain of betrayal. A page carefully removed from my journal, so I wouldn't notice. My angry, messy cursive leans across the page.

"What's this?" Johnny asks, coming up beside me.

"Nothing." I hastily refold the page, tuck it into my pocket. My face flushes. I can't look at Ryan. He must've read my words. It's as if he caught me naked.

"What do you mean, nothing?" Johnny says. "What is it?"

"She stole it," I say. "Eris did. A page from my journal."

Johnny's brows rise. He mouths "Oh." He and Ryan trade a look, then Johnny says, "What page?"

"Just . . . musings." I muster the courage to look at Ryan. "Where did you find this?"

"Among her belongings," he says. "I thought you might want it back."

"You don't need it as . . . evidence?"

"We have what we need. The page belongs to you." He holds my gaze.

"You knew it was mine. I can't believe she took it. I feel . . . violated."

"Don't blame you," Ryan says.

"Thank you," I say. "For returning it."

"No problem. It isn't anyone's to keep."

Ryan looks toward Eris's house. Johnny and I follow his gaze. Her entire property has been cordoned off as a crime scene. Two police cars sit in the driveway. Investigators are still combing through the rooms. Eris hid behind those reflective windows, watching us, waiting for her moment to slip into the cottage and steal my secrets.

While I was in the hospital, Ryan explained everything—her irrational obsession with Johnny, the laboratory evidence that linked her to Todd Severson, that identified him as the perpetrator who purchased the accelerant the night of the fire.

"Glad she's in custody," Johnny says. He takes my hand, his fingers warm and comforting.

Ryan nods at him. "The hang-ups on your cell phone. We traced them back to her."

"Crazy," Johnny says.

"Wasn't the first time," Ryan says. "We found a doc she stalked a few years ago. Before she focused on you. Wrote him letters, cards . . ."

"Shit," Johnny says.

"She wrote the card with the garlic on it, about fire as a prelude to better things," I say. "Didn't she?"

Ryan nods. "Most likely." He heads back to his truck.

I let go of Johnny's hand and follow him. "What's going to happen to her?"

"First step, arraignment. I'll keep you posted." He gets into the truck, rolls down the window, and looks at me. He and I share a strange intimacy now. He knows what I wrote about my husband, the terrible, scathing emotions.

I can feel Johnny behind me, silent, stoic.

"Have you seen the kid?" Ryan says.

"Yesterday," I say. "She's okay." At Harriet's place, Mia played quietly with her Barbie dolls, new ones we gave her. She was pensive, not saying a word. But she is alive.

"She's got a long road ahead," Ryan says. "Hard to recover from what she's been through."

"Thank you for saving her," I say.

"*You* saved her," Ryan says. "Twice now."

He pulls out of the driveway and takes off down the road, leaving nothing but a wisp of exhaust in his wake.

CHAPTER FORTY

I park at the curb on Sitka Lane, right in front of the bare land where the two demolished houses once stood. I imagine the home Johnny and I shared, the light slanting in through the windows, the hydrangeas in bloom. I imagine my wedding ring, lost in the fire. I picture Monique standing on the back deck, reaching out for the bag of charcoal, her white-blond hair shining in the twilight.

"Sarah?"

I turn to see Pedra hurrying down her driveway in jeans and a blue shirt, not her usual splashes of color. She's muted, subdued. She gives me a wordless hug, then steps back, and we look at each other. Her eyes are red and puffy from crying. She grips my arm in desperation. "Oh, Sarah."

"I got your message," I say. "Sorry it took me a while to get here."

"Did Jessie call you?"

"No. What's going on?"

Tears spill from her eyes. She wipes them away. "Come. You must see." Pedra ushers me across the street, into her house, and shows me Jessie's room, unnaturally neat, her books arranged by height on the shelves. But she left gaps, as if she couldn't bear to part with her

favorites. And she took the jewelry box and some of the lotion and perfume bottles. She lined up the remaining bottles in perfect order. She
left no clothes lying around. No sign of lace bras or thongs. But on the
bed, she left a box with a handwritten note attached. *I stole this stuff. It
belongs to Monique Kimball.*

I open the box. Inside I find Monique's pen, makeup, journal.
"You looked in here?" I say to Pedra.

She nods, sniffing.

"I'm so sorry," I say. "Do you know where she went?"

Pedra shakes her head, trembling. "The police, they say they can do
nothing. She is eighteen."

"She didn't press charges against Adrian, did she?" My heart is
sinking.

"Don tried to get her to. He went to Adrian's apartment. They're
gone. The place is empty. She talks to you—I thought she might have
called you. She's not answering her phone."

I hug Pedra again. "She didn't call. I'm sorry."

"I tried so hard. Don and I. We tried to keep her under control.
She's under that boy's spell."

"I know you're worried about her. You did everything you could.
She has to save herself. We have to hope she'll come around." I hold
on to Pedra and let her sob against my shoulder. There is nothing else
to be done.

CHAPTER FORTY-ONE

Johnny and I take the stone path at 24 Oceanview Lane. The house is unfurnished. A heavy lock on the front door prevents us from entering.

I tiptoe through the grass to the bay window. A breeze lifts my hair. The interior rooms entice me—gleaming oak floors, tile entryway, vaulted ceilings. I can see all the way back through the sliding French doors to the grassy dunes and the sunlit ocean beyond.

Johnny comes up beside me. He cups his hands against the window. "Helluva view. What do you think?"

"I have to see the inside."

He produces the key he borrowed from the Realtor, unlocks the door, and opens it. Inside, the house smells freshly painted.

Johnny heads down the spacious hallway to the bedrooms, while I linger in the foyer, touching the unopened envelope in my pocket. I barely had time to grab the mail on my way out. The box held only two items, a credit card bill and this letter. I have not yet shown it to Johnny.

"This could be your writing studio," he calls out. "When your mom gets back, she'll love the guest room."

"My mother won't stay," I say, too softly for him to hear. I walk back through the kitchen, open the sliding glass doors to the deck. The lullaby of the surf mingles with the call of seagulls. The wind rustles through the dune grasses. A silhouette of a man strolls along the beach, a black dog weaving around him.

"Did you hear me?" Johnny comes up behind me, his boots echoing on the floor.

"Loud and clear." I can also hear Natalie's voice, all the way from India. *What if there's a tsunami? You'll be way too close to the ocean.*

"You're not impressed?" he says.

"The house is lovely."

"But?"

"I don't know." About so many things. "I'm going for a walk." I head down the path across the dunes.

Johnny doesn't follow, as if he senses my need to be alone. When I reach the waterline, I pull out the letter. In the distance, long-necked cormorants ride the waves, and farther out, a freighter glides along the horizon.

I open the envelope and unfold the letter. At the top is the logo of Northwest DNA Testing Services. My fingers shake as I read on.

> Based on the DNA Analysis, the alleged Father, Jonathan McDonald, cannot be excluded as the biological Father of the Child, Mia Beaumont, because they share the same genetic markers. The probability of the stated relationship is indicated below, as compared to an untested, unrelated person of the same ethnicity.
>
> Probability Percentage: 99.9942%

The words blend together in a blur. The surf laps across my shoes, cold on my toes, but I barely notice.

Johnny is calling to me now, traipsing down across the dunes. "You okay?" he shouts. "Come on back. There's a storm coming in."

So there is. I stand poised between land and sea, past and future, the rain soaking my skin, the wind in my hair.

ACKNOWLEDGMENTS

I'm deeply grateful for all the people who've encouraged and believed in me through the years, including my relatives, my husband, my friends, and Marilyn Lundberg. A heartfelt thank-you to my brilliant editor at Amazon Publishing, Tara Parsons, amazing copy editor Ben Grossblatt, the wonderful Amazon team; and to my fabulous agent, Paige Wheeler, her assistant Ana-Maria Bonner, and their astute readers; and my outstanding foreign rights agent, Taryn Fagerness.

As always, I'm thankful for the talented and supportive authors in my writing group: Susan Wiggs, Sheila Roberts, Elsa Watson, Kate Breslin, and Lois Dyer.

To South Kitsap Fire Chief Wayne Senter (retired): thank you for spending hours on the phone with me, patiently answering my questions and relating bizarre stories from your distinguished career in firefighting. Truth really is stranger than fiction. Thank you also for reading the fire passages in the manuscript for technical accuracy, and for your support and enthusiasm.

I'm deeply indebted to the wise and experienced Maggie Crawford, editor extraordinaire, who guided me through developmental revisions and pushed me to do my best.

Thanks to Rich Penner and Stephen Messer, who read versions of my opening chapters and offered useful feedback. To my hiking buddies Randall Platt, Dianne Gardner, Patricia Stricklin, and Elizabeth Corcoran Murray: what would I do without you? Thanks to Andrea Hurst, a great colleague, mentor, and friend. Thank you to the Friday Tea brainstorming group, including, but not limited to, Terrel Hoffman, Toni Bonnell, Carol Caldwell, Sandi Hill, Jana Bourne, Jan Symonds, and Misty McColgan (Misty gave me the great idea for the Miracle Mouse portrait). Anita and Christa LaRae, thank you for brainstorming lunches. Santhan Giarratano, thank you for brainstorming at the pool. Pets and treats for my five feline muses: Ruby, Teddy, Simon, Luna, and Tiny. You're the best furballs anyone could hope to love.

ABOUT THE AUTHOR

Carol Ann Morris ©2015

A. J. Banner illuminates the darkest corners of the human heart with her stories of suspense. Born in India and raised in Canada and California, she earned degrees from the University of California, Berkeley. An avid hiker, swimmer, and animal lover, she lives on the Olympic Peninsula in Washington State with her husband and four rescued cats.